Advance Praise for

THE TROUBLE WITH GOD

"What's the fastest way to become an atheist? Read the Bible. What's the funnest way to become a know-it-all-smartass atheist? Read Chris Matheson."

—Penn Jillette, Emmy Award–winning magician and *New York Times* best-selling author

"Chris Matheson plumbs the Bible, Koran, Book of Mormon, and the works of L. Ron Hubbard for their patent silliness, ugliness and contradictions just so we can hear God's take on it all. He is not amused—but we are."

—Robyn E. Blumner, president and CEO, Center for Inquiry

"A raucous ride, stand-up theology."

—Dan Barker, co-president, Freedom From Religion Foundation

"Chris Matheson apparently plans on uniting all the Abrahamic religions in their hatred of him. Funny as hell."

—Peter Boghossian, author, *A Manual for Creating Atheists*

"Chris Matheson's egocentric, homophobic, misogynistic, insecure, vengeful god is back and he's as hilariously wretched as ever. Matheson once again rewrites the so-called holy scriptures . . . with a brutally honest eye and his trademark raucous humor. I laughed out loud at every paragraph. Required reading for the overly pious."

—Natasha Stoynoff, *New York Times* best-selling author

THE TROUBLE WITH GOD

THE TROUBLE WITH GOD

*A Divine Comedy about Judgment
(and Misjudgment)*

Chris Matheson

PITCHSTONE PUBLISHING
Durham, North Carolina

Pitchstone Publishing
Durham, North Carolina
www.pitchstonepublishing.com
Copyright © 2018 by Chris Matheson

10 9 8 7 6 5 4 3 2 1

Library of Congress Cataloging-in-Publication Data

Names: Matheson, Chris, author.
Title: The trouble with God : a divine comedy about judgment (and
    misjudgment) / Chris Matheson.
Description: Durham, North Carolina : Pitchstone Publishing, [2018]
Identifiers: LCCN 2017060263| ISBN 9781634311502 (hardcover) |
    ISBN 9781634311519 (epub) | ISBN 9781634311526 (pdf) | ISBN
    9781634311533 (Mobi)
Subjects: LCSH: God—Attributes—Fiction. | BISAC: FICTION /
    Humorous. | FICTION / Religious. | GSAFD: Humorous fiction. | Bible
    fiction. | Satire.
Classification: LCC PS3613.A8262 T76 2018 | DDC 813/.6—dc23
LC record available at https://lccn.loc.gov/2017060263

To my father

GLOSSARY

Old Testament (OT)

Gen.—Genesis
Ex.—Exodus
Lev.—Leviticus
Deut.—Deuteronomy
Jud.—Judges
1S—I Samuel
2S—II Samuel
1K—I Kings
2K—II Kings
Job—Book of Job
Ecc.—Ecclesiastes
Song—Song of Songs
Isa.—Isaiah
Ezek.—Ezekiel
Dan.—Daniel
Jon.—Jonah

New Testament (NT)

Mat.—Matthew
Mar.—Mark
Lu.—Luke
Jo.—John
Acts—The Acts
Gal.—Galatians
2T—II Timothy
Rev.—Revelation

Koran (K)

2—The Cow
3—The Family of Imran
4—The Women
5—The Feast
6—The Cattle
7—Wall Between Heaven and Hell
15—Al-Hijr
16—The Bees
17—The Children of Israel
19—Mary
21—The Prophets
22—The Pilgrimage
23—The True Believers
25—The Criterion
26—The Poets
27—An-Naml
33—The Allied Troops
34—Sheba
35—The Originator
37—Who Stand Arrayed in Rows
38—Sad
45—Kneeling
47—Muhammad
54—The Moon
55—Ar-Rahman
76—Time
90—The Earth
98—The Clear Proof
109—The Unbelievers
111—Abu Lahab
114—Men

Book of Mormon (BOM)

1N—1 Nephi
2N—2 Nephi
Jac.—Jacob
Mos.—Mosiah
Al.—Alma
Hel.—Helaman
3N—3 Nephi
4N—4 Nephi
Mor.—Mormon
Eth.—Ether

Dianetics

TC—The Clear
TRM—The Reactive Mind
TCATO—The Cell and the Organism
TD—The "Demons"
PD—Preventive Dianetics
TMP—The Mind's Protection
P-SI—Psycho-Somatic Illness
PEAB—Prenatal Experience and Birth
COA—Contagion of Aberration
K-ITE—Keying-in the Engram
ROC—Release or Clear
TLOR—The Laws of Returning
EATLF—Emotion and the Life Force
STOE—Some Types of Engrams
MAAOT—Mechanics and Aspects of Therapy
RTFCATTT—Returning, the File Clerk and the Time Track
D-PAF—Dianetics-Past and Future

CHAPTER ONE

God walks through heaven.

His footsteps echo. Heaven is deserted and he is alone again, exactly as he was at the start. Or, that is, almost alone. Not quite. He's working on it.

It is dead silent and very bright. It's never dark in heaven. (NT, Rev. 22:5) Because it's always so bright, God never sleeps well and he is often tired. Also, he is hungry. Earth ceased to exist a long time ago. God wants a grilled steak, but there are none. There is nothing to eat. He feels like he is slowly starving.

What year is it? It's hard to say. "Time" officially ended with Judgment Day, which occurred, what? Twenty years earlier? Fifty? One hundred? God honestly can't tell anymore.

God is headed for a place he calls "The Big Bridge." Once it had connected two beautiful parts of heaven, linking a flowery meadow to a pristine lake. Now the flowers are all dead and the lake is dry and cracked. Everything in heaven is both overgrown and dead; first it grew uncontrollably, then it died. But God is glad the lake is gone. He's always hated water.

If God is lucky, there will be dozens of angels clumped underneath the Bridge, hanging upside down like bats. After especially crazed periods of violence, during which the angels would attack and kill each other for weeks at a time, lopping each other to bits with their massive swords, they would finally need to rest. These were the times when God could most successfully exterminate them.

He'd created far too many angels, God now conceded to himself. "I didn't actually need *two hundred million* of them. (NT, Rev. 9:16) Two million would have been more than enough to butcher mankind. I got by with a *handful* of angels for a long time, why did I think I needed two hundred million?" Once the angels had turned against God (which they had, of course, because in the end *everything* turned against God, nothing and no one could be trusted), God had started hunting them down and destroying them. When God was honest with himself, however, he had to admit that his angels hadn't been trustworthy almost from the start. How long had they even existed before they were sneaking down to Earth and having sex with human women, who then gave birth to freaky oversized children? (OT, Gen. 6:4) "I didn't create you to fly down and have sex with whores!" God had screamed at a few of the angels. "That's pretty much the exact *opposite* of why I created you, in fact!" The resulting angel-human hybrids had been goggle-eyed monstrosities. "Zamzummims," the Ammonites had called them. (OT, Deut. 2:20) "Kill the Zamzummims," they'd shrieked as they giddily chased the spindly creatures off of cliffs.

God had managed to kill 99.9% of his angels by now. Smallpox had been extremely effective; angels had zero immunity to it. Quicksand had also worked surprisingly well. Angels had idiotically walked right into it, then slowly been sucked down and died. Or, to be honest, "died." All that *really* happened to them was that they were sent down to hell where they were ruled over by God's archenemy, Satan. That was another flaw in his plan, God now conceded. *Next* time things would be different, he vowed to himself. *Next* time, there would be justice. *Next* time people would get what they *deserved*. (This thought both excited and unsettled God; he was never sure why.)

God is down to the last few hundred angels now, but these final survivors do seem to be *slightly* more intelligent than the rest. Angels in general are extremely stupid creatures—"like psychotic male models," God has often said. Lately, a group of angels has been flying closer to God's palace, hovering menacingly over it and staring balefully down at him. It's time to take them out.

Crossing the Big Bridge, God moves stealthily. Angels sleep lightly. If they hear him approaching they will instantly stir and fly away and he might only get a few of them. He wants to finish this group off. Making a sharp right turn, God starts down a steep little trail that winds its way to what had once been a lush creek bed but is now hard like concrete. Reaching the bottom, God turns and looks up. There they are, a thick clump of angels, sleeping with their wings wrapped around themselves like cloaks.

Bracing himself, God raises his arms upward. An angel stirs and gazes blankly down at him, its eyes inky and cold. Nearby, other angels slowly begin to move. God suddenly thrusts his hands upward forcefully and begins to shoot fire out of them, bathing the angels with flames. As angels sizzle and burn, flapping and fluttering to their deaths all around him, God steps over their charred bodies and continues firing upward.

Angels fly like massive hawks. It takes them a moment to get airborne, but once they do, they are expert fliers. You have to get them early or they will escape you. God speeds up his pace now, fire-blasting as many angels as he can. Because angels are "ethereal beings," what falls on God is something like wet, pink confetti. It smells terrible, though; "Like rotten eggs mixed with dog feces," is how God puts it. God sprays a final massive burst of fire at the roof of the bridge, then stops. Everything is silent and still for a long moment. "Have I gotten them all?" God wonders.

Then a hand slowly emerges from a hidden crevice; it is followed by a large black wing. An angel, who has been hiding in the crack, quickly unfolds itself and stares down at God. "*Gabriel*," God whispers to himself. Once Gabriel had been his favorite angel, his ally and messenger (OT, Dan. 9:21, NT, Lu. 1:11), the one whom God had trusted enough to send down to talk to . . . but no, never mind her, God didn't want to think about her and he wouldn't.

Gabriel gazes down at God expressionlessly. A moment passes between them. God suddenly raises his arms again and fires. Gabriel is a brilliant flier, though; he easily dives and twists out of the way, then swoops down and suddenly lands directly before God, his massive sword raised.

God falls back onto the ground, fires up at Gabriel again. But Gabriel is elegant, nimble. He dodges the flames once more. He lifts his giant sword high, about to bring it down on his creator. But just as the sword drops, God rolls out of the way and kicks violently, connecting with Gabriel's lower leg and knocking him off balance. As the angel wobbles, God takes advantage of the opening to leap to his feet and knock the sword out of Gabriel's hand. God lunges forward, seizes Gabriel by the throat and begins to squeeze. Gabriel is athletic but God is strong. Pressing his powerful body against Gabriel to prevent the angel from raising his wings, God squeezes harder. Gabriel struggles—his face turns red, then blue, then white. Gabriel is dead.

God lets the limp body drop heavily to the ground. He looks down at it, hesitates, then kicks it—and kicks it again—and again—and yet again—until he is exhausted and completely out of breath.

Staring down at Gabriel's motionless body, a question suddenly crosses God's mind: *"How did I end up here?"*

And with that question, his mind drifts backward.

CHAPTER TWO

One problem, the biggest one probably, right from the very start, had been women. "I never *ever* should have created them," God curses under his breath, now slowly trudging back toward his distant palace. "Why on Earth did I create woman out of *myself*? I never should have done that, *never*." (OT, Gen. 1:27) God stops, considers for a moment, vigorously shakes his head. "And you know what, I actually *didn't*. I made *man* in my own image, that's perfectly true, but NOT *woman* and do you know why? Because *I'm not a woman*, okay? (I shouldn't even have to say that, *obviously* I'm not a woman.) No, I made man and then, and only after seeing whether he could be satisfied with the company of animals (OT, Gen. 2:18–19), did I make woman. Out of him. *Him*, not me. I tried to spare the man, when you think about it. 'Be happy with the animals, Adam,' I was trying to tell him. 'Don't make me bring woman into this world because she will be far tougher than you, filled with hidden dangers which you will never fully grasp; believe me when I tell you that she will inevitably destroy you.'" (One thing that *had* caused God to feel occasional pangs of guilt over the years was having left

Adam alone with the animals for perhaps a *bit* too long. "Poor goat," God murmured every single time he witnessed human-goat sex in years to come, which was a lot. On the other hand, God comforted himself, *some* of those goats had obviously been begging for it [OT, Lev. 20:15–16], and *those* goats God didn't feel sorry for one little bit—they had been slutty goats who deserved to be stoned and then barbecued.)

Stopping for a moment, halfway up a rocky hill, a question occurs to God: "Why didn't I *start* with a woman and then impregnate her? I *knew* I was going to do that at some point, why not at the very beginning? Wouldn't that have made more logical sense than starting with a man, surgically removing his rib and then essentially 'cloning' a woman from it? Also, why did I place the 'seeds' for the woman in the man's *rib?* Wouldn't it have been easier to put them in his fingernails or his hair?" God was not a trained surgeon and because all he'd had was a sharp rock, the man had nearly bled out because removing *one* rib? It's not that easy, okay? But the hardest part of the procedure had turned out to be "speed-growing" Eve from a single bone. (OT, Gen. 2:22) "Who grows something out of a *bone*, you know what I'm saying?" God later asked Gabriel.

Adam had looked elated when God had led Eve over to him. "She is made of my bones!" he had cried happily (which God had found overt and literal), followed by "I will call her 'woman' since from 'man' was she taken" (which God had found pretentious). "A man leaves his mother and father and goes with his wife," *someone* had then announced. (OT, Gen. 2:23–24) "At first I wasn't sure who had said it," God later recalled, "but then I decided that it pretty much had to have been Adam because why would *I* talk about 'leaving the father'? I definitely wouldn't." It was a presumptuous thing for Adam to have said, though, God remembered thinking. "You're not the one who makes the rules around here, okay, Adam? Also, what are you even *talking* about?

You had no mother. Maybe you *wish* you had one, maybe we all wish that, but that doesn't mean we actually did!"

"Next time," God tells himself, starting up the rocky hill again, "I will do things very differently." (It went without saying, by the way, that there would be a next time. Reality was *eternal,* after all. No matter how much God wished that it would end . . . well, it wouldn't. It would go on forever because that was obviously the way God had made it, even if he had no idea why anymore. Other than eternal punishment, that is; there was always that.)

"*Next* time," God mutters to himself, "there will be no *women!*" Female animals, yes, fine, but no female humans. "Think about it: If Eve doesn't show up, does Adam betray me?" God shakes his head decisively. No way. Adam was a weakling; he'd have stayed in line. "*Next* time," God announces, "I will create a limited number of men who I will allow to eat from the Tree of Life and thereby live forever. *However,*" God quickly adds to himself, "I will *not* permit the unholy allure of homosexuality to take hold of them. (OT, Gen. 19:4–9) *These* men will not be so damned interested in penises and balls!" God's "garden-men," as he liked to call them (and there wouldn't be many of them, by the way, twenty at most), would work quietly in the Garden of Eden for all eternity, while the rest of the earth stayed completely empty. Twenty male virgins in white robes with God's name tattooed in big block letters on their foreheads, gardening quietly forever, yes, now *that* sounded perfect. "No women," God grumbles to himself. "No women *at all.*"

But let's be honest. Women hadn't been the only problem for God. No, men had been a problem too—specifically, God's men—more specifically, his supposed *friends.* "They were all disloyal, every damned one of them," God growls under his breath. Solomon, for instance, had been almost like a son to God. "That's how I looked at him, it truly is," God recalls. (OT,

2S 7:8) Their friendship had begun when Solomon had asked God for the ability to know good from evil. (OT, 1K 3:9–12) This was a privilege that God had never given to anyone, right from the Tree of Knowledge onward. God hadn't *wanted* humans to possess this kind of wisdom. He hadn't wanted humans to possess wisdom of any kind, when you got right down to it. (That had been the basic problem with the Tower of Babel, by the way. By working together, humans might have done *amazing* things. They might have invented—who knows? Electricity . . . automobiles . . . even computers! Since God didn't want any of those things to happen, he had to split mankind up. [OT, Gen. 11:6] Also, God had an additional *tiny little* problem with Babel which pertained to his foreknowledge that in time it would turn into a seed-guzzling whore of a city called Babylon!) Because God had liked Solomon so much, however, he had decided to give him the deep insight he asked for. "I gave him wisdom as vast as the grains of sand on a beach, which is a lot, okay? Maybe not *infinite*, like mine, but a lot. I made him smarter than all of the Egyptians put together and fine, Egyptians are basically idiots, but still, I'm talking about literally *all* of them put together!" (OT, 1K 5:9–10)

CHAPTER THREE

At first, God had strongly approved of what Solomon did with his great intelligence. God had frankly *adored* the Temple Solomon built for him. (OT, 1K 6:12–13) Solomon used a lot of gold and God dug that. (God had always loved gold and worn a lot of gold jewelry: He had several thick rings and a chunky bracelet, not to mention a heavy gold crown and, on occasion, some toerings.) Solomon had also included plenty of pomegranates in the design of the Temple, which had thrilled God, who'd always had a deep appreciation for pomegranates. (OT, Ex. 39:25) "I *knew* pomegranates would look marvelous and they *do!*" he had exulted.

The first sign that Solomon was going off-track had come with the big speech he gave when the Temple opened. "Why is he putting *pressure* on me?" God had instantly wondered. "Why is he saying 'Those promises you made, you better *keep* them, God?' (OT, 1K 8:25–26) Because what if I *don't*? (And guess what, I *won't*.)" Then the speech had gotten worse. Solomon had started implying that nonbelievers, even believers in *other* gods, deserved God's love and support; that God somehow "owed" it to people to forgive their sins because, you know, "*everybody* sins."

(OT, IK 8:46) "That is certainly true," God had thought. "And *that* is why everybody gets punished!"

"What is Solomon trying to *do* here?" God had fumed, listening to him speak. "Is he trying to imply that perhaps *other* people are partially correct in their beliefs? (OT, 1K 8:39) That perhaps no one possesses 'absolute truth'? That maybe many humans get glimpses of the truth and that it's only by putting all of these glimpses together that they might see the larger truth? Because if that's what he's trying to suggest, then all I can say is *BULLSHIT!* There is one truth and it's *mine* and you are *not* going to 'enlarge' my story here, Solomon!"

Solomon had made up for some of his presumptuous speechifying by barbecuing 142,000 cows and sheep immediately afterward. (OT, 1K 8:63) To say that it had smelled delicious would be a vast understatement. God had sat for hours up in the sky, inhaling deeply and murmuring "mmmm-*mmmm*" to himself. Solomon had also offered God a bunch of fat and God had definitely appreciated that. (OT, 1K 8:64) "Why do I love fat so much?" God had asked himself on more than one occasion. "Other than for the candle-making, I mean."

Solomon's Temple speech had been so nettlesome to God that not long afterward he had appeared to Solomon in a dream. (OT, 1K 9:2) (It was a sex dream, needless to say. Solomon was, to be blunt, *obsessed* with bush. And not the burning kind either, no, the unclean, bleeding kind!) In the dream, God had leveled with Solomon. "If you don't behave yourself, I will *wipe you out,*" God had announced. "All your wealth and power will evaporate and before long everyone will be asking '*What did he do that was so bad?*' And do you know what the answer will be, Solomon? '*He turned on God,*' that's what."

"What was the first commandment I *ever* gave?" God remembered asking Gabriel at the time. "I mean, honestly, what were the first *three*? 'Do *not* worship any gods other than me,' right?" (OT, Gen. 20:2–5) So what did Solomon do? He started flirting with other gods, including my (imaginary, *definitely* imaginary) arch-nemesis, the sex-god, Baal!" Solomon had ended up marrying, among others, Pharaoh's daughter. To repeat: Solomon married *Pharaoh's daughter.* "You built a *palace* for her, Solomon? (OT, 1K 9:24) What the hell were you thinking?! I *loathe* Pharaoh! I spent a good chunk of time mind-effing Pharaoh back in the day, that's how much I hated him! (OT, Ex. 7:1–14:30) Did you pay *any* attention to what I told you in that dream, or were you too caught up in your little 'threesome' to even remember it?"

Watching the Queen of Sheba play on Solomon's ego, God had shaken his head in mortified disbelief. "Oh, you're so incredibly *wise*, Solomon," the Queen had cooed. "I didn't believe it was *possible*, but you're even *wiser* than people said you were. And ooooohhh, you're so *rich.*" (OT, 1K 10:6–7) And the Queen of Sheba had just been the start. After her had come a *parade* of nonbelieving women, basically one whore after another until Solomon eventually had a *thousand* women in his life. (OT, 1K 11:3)

"I'm still not sure why I didn't have Solomon killed," God thinks to himself, now entering a forest of dead, grey trees. Solomon had whored around, flirted with God's (imaginary— *imaginary!*) enemy, Baal; he had *mocked* God. If there was one person on Earth whom God would have been fully justified in killing, it was Solomon. But for some reason, he hadn't been able to bring himself to do it. "He betrayed me in the worst possible ways and all I could do was say, 'I'm going to give your kingdom to your *servant* after you're dead, Solomon'? That was my big threat? Quickly followed by: 'Oh, but don't feel *too* bad about it, because, you know, not your *whole* kingdom, Solomon, no, some of it I will give to your *son*'"? (OT, 1K 11:11–13)

Solomon's son Rehoboam, by the way, had turned out to be an idiot, the kind of man who brags about the size of his own penis. ("I have never ever felt the need to do that," God proudly murmurs to himself. "And that is because I am extremely confident in that department. There is no problem there, believe me, *believe me*.") Rehoboam had also allowed for the presence of *male whores* near the Temple, which had infuriated God. (OT, 1K 14:24) "That ... is ... an ... OUTRAGE," God had sputtered in rage as he watched those pretty boys parading their firm buns outside his Temple.

God remembered feeling extremely bitter during this stretch of time against Solomon—definitely, for his disloyalty—but even more so against women, because of the way they had seduced and therefore ruined his old friend and surrogate son. God had looked for a woman to take his rage out on—and Jezebel had fit the bill perfectly. God had watched Jezebel's death again and again, sometimes slowing it way down, sometimes even studying it frame by frame. (God recorded everything, pretty much, on a kind of, well, proto ... *something*. "I'm not a tech guy, never was.") There Jezebel had stood, looking like the whore she was, all made-up, with her hair done, dressed in finery. God had had some eunuchs ("See how well your feminine charms work on them") push Jezebel out a window. It was quite a drop and she had landed like a bag of ripe tomatoes, splat, her blood spraying everywhere. (OT, 2K 9:33) Wonderfully visual.

Then—and this had been great, God had been quite proud of this—he'd had some horses (geldings obviously, for the exact same reason as the eunuchs) trample Jezebel's body. "Step on her head, step on her HEAD!" God had yelled down at the horses, but they hadn't done it because earth horses don't like to step on things like human heads if they can possibly help it. (Heavenly horses, on the other hand, love to step on human heads; they laugh while they do it, "Hahaha.") The sound of Jezebel's bones snapping and cracking as the horses stomped on her had been *classic*. God had then had Jezebel chopped up into pieces: "Separate her head, feet, and hands!" he had cried down to his people. "As for the rest of her"—and oh my goodness, this had been *outstanding*—"Feed her to the dogs!" After all the frustrations surrounding Solomon's betrayal of him and the subsequent super-messy breakup of Israel, God had needed a good laugh, and watching a bunch of dogs taking dumps the next day had definitely provided it. "How you feeling *now*, Jezzy?" God had jeered as he watched the dogs pooping her out. (OT, 2K 9:36–37)

But the truth was that the end of the friendship with Solomon had been very hard on God. He had felt hurt, betrayed, and extremely angry. "I was so enraged that I wanted to see children not only eaten by bears (OT, 2K 2:23), but also smashed on rocks, slashed to pieces, and cut out of their mother's bellies!" (OT, Isa. 13:16–18) God had felt a tiny bit uneasy about all this child-killing stuff. At the very least, it hadn't *sounded* good and he knew that. But remember: All those murdered children had been *innocents* and therefore immediately after they were disemboweled or smashed to bits on rocks or yanked out of their mother's bellies or gobbled up by she-bears or, you know, *whatever*, they had joined God in heaven. Now granted, that had turned out to be weird too, because the children had invariably arrived in heaven in an extremely traumatized state and they had screamed endlessly and that's why before long God had had to send most of them (okay, all of them) down to hell. "But the *plan* was for them to be in heaven with me, it just didn't work out that way is all."

CHAPTER FOUR

But the *worst* thing Solomon had done to God, the betrayal that God had never been able to get out of his mind, the one that had really *stuck,* was the way he had made God look like a complete buffoon in his dreadful Book of Job. "People said they weren't sure who wrote Job but look at the similarities to Ecclesiastes, both linguistically and thematically!" God had thought to himself. "'Oh, life is so pointless, life is so ridiculous!' They were both *obviously* written by Solomon!"

Had Job *generally* been a true story? Yes, obviously. There certainly had been a man named Job whom God had allowed Satan to torture in order to prove a point and win a bet. In the end, yes, God had yelled down at Job from heaven and berated him, that part was true too. But beyond those rudimentary facts, well, the picture that Solomon drew of God in Job was *all* wrong. "I can easily refute so many things that Solomon wrote!" God thinks to himself. And as he pushes deeper into the dead, dark forest, he proceeds to do exactly that.

Question One: "When I asked Satan where he'd been near the beginning of the story, did I not already know the answer?" (OT, Job 1:6)

Refutation: "Of course I knew! I'm God; I know everything! Satan had been on Earth plotting against me, exactly as I wished him to! I was simply being *polite.* 'Where have you been?' was my standard question at the time, sort of, you know, a variation on 'How have you been?'"

Question Two: "Was it 'senile' of me to repeat the *exact* same question to Satan the second time I saw him?" (OT, Job 2:2)

Refutation: "Not in the least! Look, just because I sometimes repeated myself, that in no way implies that I was 'senile.' There's *a lot* to remember when you're the creator of the entire universe, so fine, sometimes I *did* repeat myself a little. (OT, Deut. 14:21, Ex. 23:18–19, Ex. 34:24–26) Or sometimes maybe even kind of a lot. (OT, Ex. 20:1–4, Deut. 5:6–18) So what? Next question!"

Question Three: "Was I a 'bad loser'?"

Refutation: "Absolutely not and here's why: Because I didn't lose! The bet with Satan was whether Job would 'blaspheme' me to my face (OT, Job 1:11), and guess what, Job never *spoke* to me face-to-face, so he never had the *chance* to blaspheme me to my face and that, I think, is THAT."

Question Four: "Was it really necessary for all of Job's children to be killed for the bet? Wasn't that, you know, a bit *much*?"

Refutation: "This is absurd. For one thing, I *replaced* all of Job's children in the end. (For what it's worth, I made his new daughters much hotter than his old ones had been.) (OT, Job 42:15) Also—come on—those children died quickly, okay? Have you ever stepped on a locust? It's fast, right? It's like *crunch,* and it's over for them. Well, a whole *house* fell on Job's children. Meaning, crunch, they were like locusts. The truth is, if it had been *me* doing the punishing rather than Satan, I'd have probably made Job *eat* his children. (OT, Lev. 26:22–29) (I'd also probably have given him severe hemorrhoids, which is something I am an expert at.") (OT, 1S 5:6–12)

Question Five: "Given that Job's camels were merely stolen, couldn't I have gotten them back for the poor man in the end?" (OT, Job 1:17)

Refutation: (And God *hated* this question for its nasty, unspoken implication, i.e., that he was some kind of "poser," or "empty suit.") "I obviously *could have* gotten those stolen camels back. I can stop the sun—I *made* the sun! The idea that I'm so feckless that I couldn't even track down a few stolen camels is insulting and laughable! I simply didn't *feel* like doing it, that's all."

Question Six: (And this is where God generally started to tense up a little bit) "Have I actually walked along the bottom of the ocean?" (OT, Job 38:16)

Refutation: "Technically, no, but I obviously know what's down there, alright?!"

Question Seven: "When I said that lightning talks to me, did I mean that literally?" (OT, Job 38:35)

Refutation: "Damn right I meant it literally! Lightning literally tells me 'I am ready.' What is so hard to understand about *that*?"

Question Eight: "When I asked Job if he knew when mountain goats gave birth, did I not realize that Job probably *did* know the answer to that question?" (OT, Job 39:1–3)

Refutation: "Well, I hoped he did! We'd been talking about animals a lot and I suddenly wondered, 'When *do* mountain goats give birth?' and so I asked him. *Next!*"

Question Nine: "Do I genuinely believe that horses can't be frightened?" (OT, Job 39:22–25)

Refutation: (God was getting tired of these inane questions by now.) "Look, I *made* horses, okay? I am well aware that they are prey animals and therefore easily frightened. When I said that horses could not be frightened, I was talking about *heavenly* horses, who love battles and charge right into them, laughing 'hahahahaha' as they do; *that's* who I was talking about! (I have no idea why I should have to defend any of this anymore!")

Question Ten: "What exactly is my deal with Leviathan?"

Refutation: (This was the question that God was *most* sensitive about. He loved his pet sea monster, Leviathan, and felt extremely protective of him. [OT, Job 40:32] That's why God had by this time printed up a sheet of paper, meant to set things straight, from which he now stopped and read:)

"FOUR FACTS ABOUT LEVIATHAN, BY GOD."

1) "I absolutely *could* put a ring through his nose if I wanted to. (OT, Job 41:2) I haven't done it, but I definitely could!"

2) "Leviathan certainly *does* speak to me in a soft and pleading little voice. (OT, Job 41:3) 'Please make me your slave, Lord,' he occasionally whimpers."

3) "I unquestionably *could* tie Leviathan up so that my little girls could play with him. (OT, Job 41:5) Again, I'm not saying I *have* (the truth is I don't *have* any little girls and why would I?), I'm simply saying I *could*. And do you know why? Because sea monster or not, I am *way* tougher than Leviathan, that's why!"

4) "Of course Leviathan wears clothes (OT, Job 41:13) and has doors in his face!" (OT, Job 41:14)

Finishing, God stuffs the paper back into his robe pocket and relaxes for a moment, feeling satisfied that he has set the record straight regarding Job. Then, horribly, out of the blue, an inner voice whispers to him:

"*Solomon mocked you,*" the voice says.

"*Stop.*" God speaks aloud, forcefully. He hates this voice, always insinuating things that are not true, that God *knows* are not true. (Sometimes it feels as if Satan has snuck into God's brain and corrupted some small part of it. Which is absurd, obviously, because Satan does not have anything like that kind of power.)

"*You made Solomon smart enough to see things and he laughed at you,*" the inner voice continues.

"STOP IT, DEVIL."

"His high intelligence only led him to doubt."

"ENOUGH!"

"Only stupid people believe in you."

"SILENCE, ABOMINATION!!"

There is silence for a moment. Then the voice whispers, *"She* didn't even believe in you."

"NO!"

"She knew the truth."

God sees a crack of light, the exit from this spectral forest, and as he starts for it, *"Mary"* crosses his mind.

"No," God says aloud. "I don't want to think of her—no, *no!"*

"Mary."

CHAPTER FIVE

When God had first seen her, she was alone, walking down a street, dressed plainly and simply, her eyes lowered. She was sweet and lovely and God quickly fell for her. "Like Michael Corleone with that pretty little Italian girl in *The Godfather* who later got blown up in the car, sad," as God much later described it to Gabriel. (God was one of the very few people who understood that *Godfather III* was the true classic in the series.)

God had soon found that he couldn't stop thinking about Mary. He had found himself gazing down at her hour after hour, beginning to experience feelings he had never known before. "She is exquisite," God had thought to himself, watching while she slept, studying her lovely mouth, her soft skin, and when she stirred, her beautiful, soulful brown eyes.

One day God had finally realized something important: "I want her," he had thought. "I *desire* her."

Exhausted from his long, vaguely scary walk through the forest of skeletal trees, God now sits on the ground and absently strokes his beard. "I wanted a *real* son," he thinks to himself. "Not an adoptive one like Solomon had been, but an actual, biological one." Before seeing Mary, God had been unsure *how* he wanted to create this son, however. Should he make him out of mud, or perhaps out of one of his ribs, he had wondered? After seeing Mary, though, God understood *precisely* how he wanted to create Jesus. "I have walked the earth," he thought. (OT, Gen. 3:8) "I have eaten food." (OT, Gen. 18:7) "I have even beaten a man up." (OT, Ex. 4:24) "What I have never experienced is that which would seem to be the most sublime physical pleasure of all, lovemaking." Also, to be completely honest, God had felt for quite a long time slightly jealous of that (imaginary—*imaginary)* prick, Baal, who had clearly had a *ton* of sex. "While here I am, the eternal virgin. Well, guess what, that's about to end!"

By the time God sent Gabriel down to inform Mary about what was going to happen to her, he had known *exactly* what he wanted his angel to say. "First of all, tell Mary how *incredibly* lucky she is—blessed, use the word *blessed*—that I have chosen her. (NT, Lu. 1:28) After that, she may be unsure, or even troubled. Tell her not to be frightened, Gabriel. Tell her that I, God, really like her. Tell her that I intend to fill her womb with a baby whom she will name 'Jesus.' Tell her that Jesus will be great and that he will rule over my people, you know, basically forever." (NT, Lu. 1:31)

"If Mary asks *how* this is going to happen," God had continued, "given that she is a virgin—because she is *definitely* a virgin, Gabriel, even though she is married, she is a married virgin, because they are quite common, it turns out—anyway, as I was saying, if she asks how this will happen, given her virginity, tell her that I will come upon her!" (NT, Lu. 1:35)

"Correction, Gabriel," God had then said. "I do not intend to 'come upon' Mary, as that would be defeating my purpose, quite obviously. Tell her that . . . yes, this is very good . . . tell her that 'the power of the Highest' (and make sure that she understands that 'Highest' is capitalized if at all possible) shall *overshadow* her." God had hesitated once again at this point. "Does that sound 'rapey,' Gabriel?" God had asked, then quickly answered his own question. "Of course it doesn't. It sounds forceful—*confident*. I am God the Highest and I will *overcome* her with my power, yes, that's magnificent, say that. (Also, and this isn't *that* important, Gabriel, but if you get a chance, please ask Mary whether she and her sister are *both* named Mary. Because if they are . . . well, it's highly unimaginative of their parents, that's all I can say!") (NT, Jo. 19:25)

As God waited for what he called the "Big Night" to arrive, he found himself beginning to imagine what it would be like to actually have Mary as his girlfriend. "Maybe I wouldn't *need* the love of all mankind," he mused. "Maybe *her* love could heal me. I'm actually beginning to consider the possibility that it could!" (Of course it goes without saying that deep inside God had known that things wouldn't go this way; that Mary wouldn't love or comfort him; that she wouldn't make him feel better at all; that she would, in fact, make him feel much, much worse.)

By the time God, dressed in his finest white robe, hair and beard neatly brushed, had been flying down to meet Mary, one thing had become undeniable: He was *extremely* nervous. What if things didn't go well, God had wondered? He had never been particularly good at this sort of thing: small-talk, flirtation, whatever you wanted to call it. Frankly, he was awkward, lacking in social skills. Also, God suddenly wondered, why had he made himself an *old man* anyway, rather than, say, a twenty-five-year-old? (The answer to that one turned out to be obvious. Because old men were the very best thing to be, that's why!)

Entering Mary's room, God suddenly felt—there is no other word for it—terrified. He stood there in the doorway for a long moment before slowly crossing to Mary's small bed. God later remembered feeling flushed as he sat down. He and Mary sat together on her bed for several long, uncomfortable minutes. God stared silently at Mary, then looked away. She gazed at the floor. A candle flickered, a donkey milled around outside, some insects buzzed.

Then Mary closed her eyes, took a deep breath and lay back on the bed. God gazed down at her. "It's time," he thought to himself.

A few moments later and . . . well, it was actually happening . . . and God felt . . . amazed. "This is *wonderful*," he thought to himself. "This is . . . *sublime.*"

Mary was so beautiful . . . the sweet smell of her . . . the soft *feel* of her . . . her delicate skin and her sweet face and her feminine body and yes . . . oh yes . . . to be *touched by her.*

"She feels me," God realized with a start. "She *feels* me." It was at that moment that God began to feel extremely self-conscious. He began to smell himself . . . hear himself . . . feel himself.

"*Stop it,*" God quickly thought. "Stop thinking these awful, negative thoughts." But God discovered to his horror that it was, in fact, quite difficult to stop thinking such thoughts.

Now Mary had become aware of what was happening to God. Moment by moment, things were, how to say this, *deflating* for him.

"Think of something else, think of something *exciting,* you fool," God had demanded of himself. But his mind was filled with dark thoughts now, like a young, vulnerable animal surrounded by a swarm of biting insects.

God struggled manfully to make things work. But second by second, things got worse and worse until, before long, everything ended in shriveled, shrunken defeat.

God sat on the edge of Mary's bed, his back to her, deeply embarrassed. He couldn't think of anything to say. "*I'm sorry*" is what he wanted to say. "I'm sorry, Mary." But he didn't say that because, well, it wouldn't have made any sense; he was God, what did he have to be sorry for? Nothing at all. Instead, he got up and without a word walked outside. He stood for a moment in the darkness, then raised his arms over his head and flew back up to heaven.

The following night God sent Gabriel back down to Earth with, more or less, a turkey baster, and the deed was done. (It was actually *much* nicer than a turkey baster, if you must know; it was actually more like a wineskin, really, quite handsome in its own way—not like a turkey baster at all, in fact. As for the production of the seed itself, it was none of anyone's business what God thought about, nor did he feel the slightest bit of shame about it.)

In God's mind, there had been one unambiguously positive aspect of his failed relationship with Mary: Once he had laid eyes on her, he had stopped talking about penises and balls entirely. "I didn't even *mention* them in my second book," he later marveled to himself. "Why, I didn't even seem to care if men trimmed their penises anymore! I made my whole deal with Abraham contingent upon foreskins (OT, Gen. 17:10) and now I didn't even *care*! (NT, Gal. 5:6) Or actually I still *did*, I didn't like the 'dog-dick' look, it was repulsive to me, but I wasn't going to kill the whole deal just because some men didn't show off their handsome mushroom heads. That was obviously *not* the point of this whole thing—the point was much bigger than that! (I still did really like perfect balls, though; nothing could ever change that. And seed, I really liked seed a *lot*. And women were still repulsive to me. In later books—and yes, obviously there would be later books; I'd never stop trying to reach people, even though I'd never succeed!—women will barely even be *present*, ha.)"

CHAPTER SIX

When Jesus was born, God had wanted there to be a giant celebration of some sort. "I believe I'll move a star off its natural course!" he had declared. (NT, Mat. 2:9–10) (Which was not that easy to do, incidentally; stars are quite large, it turns out, and this one was several hundred quadrillion miles away from Earth so it took a shit-ton of travel and labor to do it—but hey, it was worth it in the end, it was a sensational effect.) "I will send three wise men to observe Jesus' birth, which will also be heralded by angels singing!" God had proclaimed. (Sadly, Jesus' birth-song hadn't been one of God's best; it had been kind of dashed-off actually. "Glory to God in the highest blah blah blah," that kind of boilerplate stuff. [NT, Lu. 2:14] It was a pretty tune, though, *vaguely* similar to "Can You Feel the Love Tonight" from *The Lion King*—which was one of God's favorite movies, as well as one of his favorite Broadway musicals, in case you're wondering!) (Another one of God's favorite pastimes: Sumo wrestling. "I love to watch those big boys go at it! Especially knowing how they're all going to sizzle in hell eternally afterward!")

God's splashy announcement regarding Jesus' birth had indirectly led to a bunch of children being killed (NT, Mat.

2:16), but by this time, God had definitely learned "not to sweat the small stuff," as he put it. ("And other than *my* needs, it's *all* small stuff, haha.") One thing God never *quite* figured out was why exactly he had announced Jesus' birth with such fanfare and then basically done nothing for the next thirty years. "It was like a huge, exciting circus opening, which was then followed by an hour of dead *silence*," he occasionally chided himself.

Sitting on a patch of hard, cold ground now, lazily running his fingers through some dirt, God thinks back to Jesus' childhood. "Was I an absent parent?" he wonders. "Should I have played more of a role in my son's life, *taught* him something maybe?" But God instantly rejects the thought. "First of all, I was extremely busy, and second of all—look, it's not like *Mary* was such an outstanding parent either, okay? Taking Jesus into the city, then heading home without him and not until the *next day* even realizing he was *gone?* (NT, Lu. 2:43–48) Then taking *three days* to find him, even though he was probably exactly where she left him? Kind of seemed like Mary *wanted* to lose that boy," God mutters under his breath, followed by: "He *was* kind of a little know-it-all." (NT, Lu. 2:49)

When Jesus had turned thirty ("90% of the way through his life," God remembered bragging to his angels at the time), God had finally set things in motion. Immediately after Jesus had been baptized by John the Baptist, God took the shape of a dove and landed on his son's shoulder. He then called down from heaven, "This is my beloved son and I am pleased with him." (NT, Mat. 3:16–17) God had considered having the bird say these words, but he decided they wouldn't sound as impressive coming out of a dove's mouth. (If doves could even talk, which they couldn't obviously, and God certainly wasn't going to send in a damned *parrot*. "It would have sounded comical and I wanted it to sound lofty.")

"Incidentally," God had informed Gabriel at the time, "with

regard to the silly rumor that is going around (which will, in the end, turn out to be *completely* true, but never mind that right now) that Jesus was with me in heaven from the very start, well, I think *this* moment makes it pretty obvious that he wasn't! I was basically *introducing* myself to him, alright? 'Hello, I am a bird possessed by your father, God. You are my son and I am happy with you.'" God hadn't liked the awkward moment that had occurred after he had spoken to Jesus from heaven. "It looked like he was waiting for me to make a whole speech or something, but that one sentence was all I had prepared. So he just stared blankly at dove-me for a long moment, until I flew away. It wasn't nearly as overwhelming a moment as I wished it had been."

With regard to John the Baptist, by the way, God had *loved* the guy. God had helped Mary's barren older sister, Elizabeth, get pregnant with John the Baptist in the first place. (NT, Lu. 1:7) ("Is 'barren' an unkind word to describe a woman?" God had once asked himself. "No, it's exactly right," he had quickly responded. "It means 'arid, bleak, and lifeless.'") John the Baptist (and God always referred to him as "John the Baptist," by the way, never just "John." "I sure do like the cut of that John the Baptist's jib!") had done all the right things: He had talked incessantly about God; he had demanded that people repent; he had even eaten bugs. (NT, Mat. 3:4) ("Not sure why I liked that so much," God thinks now, "but I surely did!") God had also loved it when John the Baptist had told people that they were evil trees who would soon be chopped down and tossed into the fire. (NT, Mat. 3:10) "Nice!" God had cried out loudly. "NICE!" (Jesus, by the way, had later *totally* stolen this tree-human analogy from John the Baptist and never once given him credit for it—which had been flat-out rude, if you asked God.) (NT, Mat. 7:19) God had been extremely saddened when John the Baptist had his head cut off and placed on a platter. (NT, Mar. 6:27–28) "That's *hideous*," God had seethed, watching. "And if I laughed, it was only out of surprise, because it definitely wasn't funny!"

Q: Were there things that Jesus had said and done during his time on Earth that God had liked?

A: Yes, definitely. Here was one. When Jesus had instructed his followers that "sparrows don't fall from trees without God doing it," God had nodded deeply. (NT, Mat. 10:29) "I *do* make sparrows fall out of trees," he had thought. "I make their little hearts stop, then watch them topple forward and land with a wee fluttery thud on the ground." God had been in control of killing *all* birds, in fact; it had been a surprisingly large part of his job and he had been gratified that Jesus brought it up, because it wasn't something that he frequently got credit for. "I particularly enjoyed killing *parrots*," God speaks aloud. "I always loathed their sarcastic little voices." God had also enjoyed killing owls. "Hoo hoo," the owls would ask, and God would smile tightly and whisper, "*God*, that's hoo," and the owls would instantly fall over dead.

Jesus had also scored some points for himself when he announced that he had come to Earth not in peace, but rather with a sword. (NT, Mat. 10:34) "Splendid!" God had declared upon hearing that. "Why don't you chop off someone's head with it then?!" When God had realized that Jesus had been speaking "symbolically," as was his wont, he had been bitterly disappointed. "Always hated it when he spoke symbolically," God mutters, absently drawing a cross in the dirt.

CHAPTER SEVEN

But almost as if he had been *trying* to annoy God, Jesus had invariably said or done pretty much exactly the *wrong* thing. Talking so much about the "Holy Ghost," for instance. (NT, Mat. 12:31–32) What the hell was *that* about? "There's no such thing as a Holy Ghost!" God had yelled when he first heard the term. "First of all, I despise ghosts and always have! (OT, Lev. 19:31) Why would I *create* one? Second of all, who is this 'Holy Ghost' supposed to be anyway, some kind of, what?—'invisible *presence* that fills people's souls up?' What an absurdly unprovable idea! And third, 'Holy Ghost' is an oxymoron, okay? Like 'Holy Devil' or 'Holy Woman'!" (It also wasn't even "monotheism," when you thought about it, God later realized; it was more like pantheism or polytheism or one of those other bullshit-isms that he loathed.) But had Jesus stopped talking about the Holy Ghost? No, he had not. He had kept blabbing about it all the way to the bitter end, in fact. (NT, Mat. 28:18)

And there was more. Actually having the nerve to tell his followers that *all* food was clean? (NT, Mar. 7:19) That had made God's head spin. "You're telling them that crabs, mice, and bat-birds (OT, Lev. 11:19) are clean to eat?" God had cried in disbelief.

"They are not clean to eat, bat-birds are filthy abominations and they always will be!" But Jesus' off-key remarks had continued: "Stop talking about men cutting their balls off!" God had thundered. (NT, Mat. 19:12) "Stop letting heavily menstruating women touch you!" (NT, Lu. 8:43–48) "And *definitely* stop adding new commandments! Don't you think that if I'd wanted humans to 'love their neighbors,' I would've told Moses that in the first place? (NT, Mat. 22:39) I couldn't care *less* if they love their neighbors, I want them to love ME, that's the point of this whole thing, Jesus, how can you not *see* that?"

Then—and this had been a big one—there was the whole *healing* thing. "I gave Jesus healing ability in order to prove his powers, alright, Gabriel?" God remembered saying. "'Do it twice, three times *maybe*, that'll be *more* than enough,' that's what I told him. I didn't need hundreds of sick people healed; I mean honestly, why did Jesus think I made so much sickness anyway, because I hated it so much? And once he started healing people, what did he think they were going to want from him? To be *cured*, that's what! Also—*also*—I'd *already* given mankind the cure to many diseases. Leprosy, for instance! I had made it clear that the cure for leprosy was to drip bird's blood in a circle outside the leper's house! (OT, Lev. 14:48–52) So why exactly did Jesus need to cure a disease I'd already cured?"

"Here's the thing. Jesus made the whole thing about *him*," God had later fumed to Gabriel. "It was all about 'Jesus and his magical healing powers,' when what I wanted it to be about was how *mad* I was and how mankind had better repent because I was *just about* to end the world! (Which I *was*, by the way. I simply changed my mind, that's all.) Think about it, Gabriel. What did Jesus' followers call themselves? '*Christ*-ians,' right? Not 'Lord-ians' or 'God-ians' or 'Yahweh-ians,' no, '*Christ*-ians.' How was I supposed to feel about that? I *created* this whole thing, without me, there is literally, and I mean quite literally, *nothing*, and they love Jesus more? What did I do to deserve *that*?"

Even worse than the healing thing from God's point of view, much worse in fact, had been Jesus' misguided decision to bring people back from the dead (not to mention teaching his idiot followers to do it too!) (NT, Mat. 10:7) "Does Jesus not grasp that him returning from the dead is meant to be *mind-blowing*? Does he not see how much he's lessening the impact of that moment by doing this? Does he not understand that if people are routinely coming back from the dead, that makes *his* return no big deal, like, 'Oh, look, Jesus is back from the dead,' 'Yeah, whatever, who cares, I saw three people come back just last week.'"

"*Also*," God thinks to himself, "Lazarus had been dead for four days, alright? *FOUR DAYS.* (NT, Jo. 11:17) You could smell him in heaven! I mean, fine, he did *look* funny, I won't deny that. It *did* make me laugh seeing this grey-faced zombie-man stumbling around and bumping into things and making weird gurgling noises, and yes, I *did* call Gabriel over, and yes, we *did* have tears rolling down our faces as we watched Lazarus trip over a rock and face-plant then jump up and run around in jerky little circles before toppling headfirst into a well. Damn, I'm laughing now just *remembering* it. Still though, it was definitely a bad idea."

Not long after the whole Lazarus flub, Jesus had started boasting about how glorious he was, or soon would be or, you know, *whatever.* "Who knows *what* he's talking about sometimes," God had snapped. Jesus had then yelled up to God, "Save me and glorify your name!" and God had instantly yelled back, "I have *already* glorified my name and I will glorify it again!" which he had thought sounded tremendously commanding, even if he hadn't been 100% sure what it meant. (NT, Jo. 12:28) Jesus had then referred to himself as "the Prince of the world," which God had found enormously presumptuous. (NT, Jo. 12:31)

God remembered feeling at this time that at least *part* of the problem with Jesus pertained to the version of his story that was being told by that insufferable little twat, John. "'In the beginning was the word and the word was with me and the word was me?' (NT, Jo. 1:1) Pretentious crap." And then there had been John's nauseating *coyness*. Talking about laying his head on Jesus' chest (which he had called his 'bosom,' *gay*) and then asking in that barfy, mewling little voice of his, "Who will betray you, Lord?" (NT, Jo. 21:20) "I should have made John the traitor, so I could have watched *his* guts explode instead of Judas's," God mutters to himself. (NT, Acts 1:18)

One thing that John *had* gotten right was that God and Jesus had a deeply, shall we say, *imbalanced* relationship. "Look at all the times Jesus talks about how much *I* love *him* in this gospel," God had pointed out to Gabriel. (NT, Jo. 3:35, 5:20, 8:54, 10:17, 15:9, 17:24) "A lot, right? Now look at the number of times he says that *he* loves *me*. (NT, Jo. 14:31) Once, right? It's insulting, Gabriel, it really is."

God had begun to suspect at this time that Jesus was, in some very subtle ways, criticizing him. "If you only love those who love you, what's good about *that*?" Jesus had asked his followers (NT, Lu. 6:32), and God had instantly bristled: "*I* only love those who love me. (The truth is, I don't even love them, but never mind that.) Is Jesus *judging* me for that? And what about him saying, 'Hate your father'? What the hell did he mean by *that*? (NT, Lu. 14:26) Did Jesus *hate* me? For what *possible* reason?"

It was around this time that people had started to accuse Jesus of being an overweight drunk. (NT, Mar. 11:19) God hadn't thought that Jesus was either overweight or an alcoholic, but he definitely hadn't minded hearing these things said. "The Fat Drunk," God had started to call Jesus. "What kind of nonsense is the Fat Drunk spouting *now*?" he would ask Gabriel in a faux-jocular voice. ("I'm going to kill the Fat Drunk soon," is what he had actually been thinking.)

CHAPTER EIGHT

Once God had made the decision that Jesus was going to die, he had quickly sent Moses and Elijah down to tell him what was going to happen. The two of them had flown down out of the sky and landed near Jesus and God had hoped going in that their conversation might be a little more, you know, *casual*, a little bit less rushed, that Jesus' death might come up more organically. But instead, Moses had landed and pretty much instantly blurted out, "You're going to be killed, Jesus." (NT, Lu. 9:31) Jesus, looking stunned, had stared back at Moses, speechless. The three men had stood there for a few moments in uncomfortable silence before Moses and Elijah had turned and walked away.

Seeing the horrified look on Jesus' face, God had thought, "I need to say something to him," so he quickly took the shape of a cloud (which had felt awesome, by the way; it had been way too long; God really enjoyed being a cloud) and called out, "This is my beloved son, listen to him!" He had said it loud enough for three of Jesus' nearby disciples to hear him. (These disciples, incidentally, *might* have been dreaming this entire event [NT, Lu. 9:32]; it sort of seemed like they had been, in fact . . . but you know what, no, they weren't, this all actually happened.)

Later, thinking back on how he'd cloud-spoken to Jesus, God felt slightly self-conscious. "I'd just had Moses tell Jesus that he was going to die; what was the point of my telling three disciples who *already* listened to Jesus that they should listen to him?" "That was kind of a non sequitur, wasn't it?" God had asked Moses when he returned to heaven. When Moses sort of hemmed and hawed a little too long, God beat the shit out of him again.

Then things got genuinely difficult.

The night before Jesus was going to be killed, he dropped to his knees and begged God for his life. (NT, Mat. 26:36–42, Mar. 14:35–36) God stared down at his son, feeling deeply conflicted. "Why *does* he have to die?" God suddenly asked himself. "What's the *point?*" A long moment passed, and then God suddenly exclaimed, "I'll let him live! I'll let him live for a *long* time, in fact! I'll have him travel the entire world, journey to every continent, let him spread my word *everywhere!* Who knows, maybe he will even get married and have children! How would that be a *bad* thing? It wouldn't; it would be wonderful. Grandchildren— great-grandchildren—*family*—that's what this is all about, not killing your own son, who on Earth would do *that?*"

God knew how the humans thought, obviously, how desperate they were to believe that he loved them. They would tell themselves the story that God had killed Jesus because he loved them so much, he knew that. But that was patently ridiculous. "The truth is," God had realized, "that if I *actually* cared for mankind at all, I would allow as many of them as possible to get to know Jesus. Also, if I had any positive feelings for Mary (no matter how badly she may have treated me), I would never force her to watch her own son being tortured to death, that would be . . . well, honestly, that would be hateful. The truth is, if there is *any* love inside of me, any at *all*, I will spare my son. And you know what, that's exactly what I will do! Don't cry, Jesus, I will act out of *love* now, like a father would. Don't cry, son, I will spare you!"

Eighteen hours later God stared silently down, barely blinking as he watched Jesus die. "Why have you forsaken me?" Jesus had whispered near the end. (NT, Mat. 27:46) God hadn't moved a muscle. "He knew the plan," he murmured to no one in particular. "He did know the plan."

But why had Jesus' death needed to be so damned *cruel?* Why so excruciating? Why so *humiliating*? Had Jesus really needed to be spat upon? Had he really needed to be mocked with, "If you're the son of God, why don't you fly down off your cross?" Had he *really* needed to have some naked man following him around? (NT, Mar. 14:51–52) ("What the hell was *that* about anyway?" God had demanded, but no one had known. When one angel had suggested "a proto-streaker," God quickly made that angel's eyes blow out.) "But honestly," God had wondered, "why did Jesus' life need to end like *that*? Why couldn't he have just taken poison like that irritating old prick Socrates? Why did I give Jesus the kind of death I subjected Jezebel, whom I *despised*, to?"

To cover his deep discomfort about this moment, God had suddenly glowered down at Earth and, feigning fury, caused a huge earthquake. (NT, Mat. 27:51) When that hadn't been sufficient to express his fake-rage ("My son," God had cried out; "My SON!"), he brought some skeletons to life and had them strut around Jerusalem for a while. (NT, Mat. 27:52–53) That had thoroughly terrified people, which God had liked. "You killed my beloved son, now deal with an infestation of moldy skeletons!" he had bellowed down at Jerusalem.

But there was one thing Jesus had said near the very end of his life that God had found he simply couldn't get out of his mind. "Forgive them, Father, for they know not what they do," Jesus had murmured. God hadn't known what to make of this remark; he remembered thinking that it didn't make any sense at all. "If they know not what they do, then why would they *need* forgiveness? Wouldn't the one who needs forgiveness in that case be the one who *does* know what he is doing?"

God lurches to his feet. "I don't want to think about that anymore," he tells himself. He wavers unsteadily for a moment, then starts slowly back toward his palace, which is now visible in the distance.

CHAPTER NINE

But the moments that had bothered God the most during Jesus' life had all involved his son's various interactions with Satan. Every time Jesus and Satan had connected, it had made God queasy. To start with, during the "temptations," why had Satan repeatedly implied that God was *not* Jesus' father? (NT, Mat. 4:3–6) This ugly suggestion, to be honest, had bothered God for a long time. "What *difference* does it make who Jesus is related to on *Joseph's* side?!" he had frequently thundered to Gabriel. (NT, Mat. 1:2–17) "Why is that relevant to anything? Joseph is *not* Jesus' father—I am Jesus' father!" These so-called genealogies had infuriated God. "They shouldn't even be in my book," he had fumed. "Why would anyone in their right mind think that Joseph was Jesus' father? What, just because he and Mary were *married*? 'Ohh, Mary's *husband* must be the father of her child?' It's utterly *laughable.*" (As to where all these nasty doubts regarding God's paternity had begun, the answer had been sadly obvious to God: "Mary. It had to be Mary.")

But the truth was that Jesus had made similarly annoying insinuations. "If God be glorified in the Son of Man," Jesus had announced, "God shall also glorify him in himself and shall glorify him." God's first reaction to this statement had been to snort derisively. (NT, Jo. 13:32) "What the hell does it even *mean?* The boy is talking gibberish!" But afterward, God had found himself fulminating about something else: Why did Jesus so often refer to himself as the "Son of Man?" "Stop calling yourself that, alright, Jesus? You're *not* the Son of Man; you're the Son of ME." But Jesus hadn't stopped; he had referred to himself as the "Son of Man" all the way to the bitter end (NT, Jo. 13:31) and it had basically pissed God off every single time.

It's true that Jesus' semi–non sequitur response to Satan's first temptation (S: "If you're the son of God, why don't you turn that stone into bread?" J: "Man does not live on bread alone." S: " . . . Wait, *what?*") (NT, Mat. 4:4) had made everyone in heaven laugh and cheer. But the bigger question was, why hadn't Jesus taken that opportunity to *prove* that he was God's son? "I specifically gave him the ability to do magic tricks with bread, Gabriel! (NT, Mar. 6:38–44) Why didn't he do one when Satan challenged him? In the same vein, why didn't he jump off the temple and let angels catch him when Satan suggested he do that? Okay, fine, technically there *were* no angels nearby to catch him, so Jesus would have been smashed on the rocks below, so maybe he was right to go around *that* one, but still, why didn't he at least *contradict* Satan? "I *am* the son of God, devil, stop saying that I am not or I will turn you into a *pig!*" Which was *another* thing Jesus could have done to Satan at any time, obviously. (NT, Mat. 8:32) (God had enjoyed it immensely, by the way, when Jesus had made demons pop out of people and fly into pigs; he had adored it when the demon-possessed pigs then proceeded to *drown* themselves. "Well played, son," God had nodded proudly as he watched the demon-pigs go under the water for the final time. "Beautifully played.")

But the most disturbing temptation by far from God's point of view had been Satan's final one: "Rule the world with me,

Jesus." (NT, Lu. 4:5–7) Why had Satan thought *this* would be tempting to Jesus? Why had he believed that the two of them teaming up was even a *possibility*? Work with me? *That* was Satan's temptation? It had made no sense. And yet . . . Satan *did* know how to tempt; it's basically what God had created him for. So what he said was never exactly meaningless. Had Satan known something—perhaps sensed something—in Jesus? A kind of personal ambition, a hidden desire to actually have power over the entire world? "Could Satan be right—could that be what Jesus truly wants?" God had asked himself before suddenly stopping in horror, recalling that Jesus had already openly stated that this was, in fact, *exactly* what he wanted. (NT, Mat. 25:31)

Why hadn't Jesus attacked Satan at that moment? Pushed him off the mountain or bashed his head in with a rock or at the very least punched him in the face and yelled: "You're evil and God is good and I will never *ever* partner with you, Satan, now GO STRAIGHT TO HELL!" All Jesus had said to Satan was, "It is written that thou shall serve only God." (NT, Mat. 4:10) "*That's* the only reason you're not teaming up with him?" God had sputtered. "Because it's *written* that you can't? What, if that *wasn't* written, then you'd do it?"

More dark questions had started to nag at God: Why was it that when Jesus exorcised people, the little devils who popped out had seemed to more or less *worship* him? (NT, Lu. 4:41) "Why are demons obeying Jesus? That's what I want to know!" God had demanded, staring down in stunned disbelief. Some people on Earth had even started to suggest that Jesus and Satan were partners by this time! (NT, Lu. 11:15) Why, God had even heard rumors that Jesus was planning on visiting Satan in his home, hell! (NT, Mat. 12:40) "He'd better not," God had rumbled ominously to himself. (Knowing that he would anyway, obviously.)

But the most confounding moment of all from God's point of view had come near the end, when Jesus gave a soggy piece of

bread (aka his "body") to the person who would betray him—
Judas.(NT, Jo. 13:26) ("And by the way, don't even get me *started*
on that whole 'eat my body, drink my blood' thing, Gabriel. What,
was Jesus a vampire or something? Not that vampires were real,
obviously. They were not. Giants [OT, Gen. 6:1–4], wizards [NT,
Rev. 22:15], zombies [NT, Jo. 11:44], talking horses [OT, Job
39:19–25], ghosts [OT, 1S 28:15–16], skeletons [OT, Ezek. 37:5;
NT, Mat. 27:52–53], dragons [NT, Rev. 12:3–4] and sea monsters
[OT, Job 40:15–31], yes, definitely. Vampires? No, no way.") But
the truly disturbing thing about this moment occurred just after
Judas ate the sop. At the *exact* moment Satan entered into Judas,
Jesus looked Judas in the eye and said, "Do it quickly." (NT, Jo.
13:27) And God had instantly thought to himself: "What the hell
did *that* mean?"

"Do it *quickly*?" Had Jesus been implying that God would
have dragged things out and made him suffer even *longer*? ("At
that moment, you know what, I definitely would have!") Had this
moment been a glimpse of some kind of clandestine relationship
between Jesus and Satan? Had God's man Paul been in on things
too? If he hadn't been, then why exactly had Satan *defended* Paul,
even to the point of beating up some priests and tearing their
clothes off for him? (NT, Acts 19:13)

What had been the *meaning* of this strange complicity
between Jesus and Satan? This question had weighed on God
for several hundred years, until one day he had suddenly known
the answer. "I don't think Jesus was my son," God told Gabriel.

CHAPTER TEN

"It stinks," God mutters, nearing his palace. It's the smell of rotting bodies and it's dreadful. There are dead wise men on the ground (NT, Rev. 4:10–11)—dead angels—dead eyeball-monsters. (NT, Rev. 4:7–8) This is something no one tells you about heaven: Bodies decay *very* slowly here. God has tried repeatedly to burn the bodies, but all he's ever managed to do is create a noxious cloud of black smoke that's drifted right back into his palace and made him violently ill, so he's given up.

Heading toward his grand exterior staircase, God wanders past what had once been an ice rink (NT, Rev. 4:6) but is now basically an empty dirt oval. His lion eyeball-monster lies dead on the ground, its many eyes seeming to stare up at God as he passes. He tries to avoid the eyes—but there are so *many* of them. ("Why did I give them so many eyes? It's like I can't ever get away from their gaze.") At the top of the staircase, God stops and stares dully at his palace. It is deathly still, utterly deserted. In the walkway before him is a small pile of dead wise men, their necks and bodies twisted, their faces contorted into grotesquely smiling rictuses. As God kicks them out of the way, their bones snap like twigs.

Entering his front door, God stops and cocks an ear. "Oh no," he instantly thinks to himself. "Not again." God hears footsteps racing toward him. It's only been a few days since the last appearance; they are coming closer and closer together now. The footsteps get nearer and nearer and then, suddenly rounding a corner, skidding, wild-eyed, and completely out of control, a man appears. He has shit smeared on his face and in his beard; his penis is erect and he is sprinting directly at God. "Test me, Lord," he cries out deliriously. "TEST ME!"

"*Ezekiel,*" God mutters disgustedly under his breath. He hates this man; he has for a long time. Back in the day, Ezekiel had made God sound like some kind of depraved pervert. The whole "dom/sub" thing that Ezekiel had implied existed between God and Jerusalem? That had been infuriating. "I'm going to collar you and put a ring in your nose, Jerusalem?" (OT, Ezek. 16:12) "Yeah, you like those golden dildos, don't you, whore?" (OT, Ezek. 16:17) "Fine, you have nice breasts and an attractive snatch, but you are a damned *whore,* Jerusalem?" (OT, Ezek. 16:7) God had *not* talked like that! Now it's true that he hated whores and he *definitely* thought golden dildo usage was abominable, but telling Jerusalem that it had nice tits? Absolutely not!

"The problem with 'prophets,'" God had frequently groused to Gabriel, "is that people don't realize that they're sometimes speaking for *themselves.* After I choose a prophet (and why I chose this Ezekiel whack-job I have no idea), people seem to think that every single thing they say is coming from me, but you know what, it *isn't.* Sometimes a lot of it, honestly *most* of it, is all *them.* Like Ezekiel instructing Jerusalem that it was 'the whore that *paid* rather than *got* paid' for instance? (OT, Ezek. 16:31–34) Okay fine, I actually *did* say that one because it was true, but all that 'horse-cock' nonsense? (OT, Ezek. 23:20) I used that term one time, Gabriel, *one time!*"

"Test me, Lord!" Ezekiel cries giddily, charging at God. God suddenly throws out his powerful right arm, violently slamming the base of his palm into Ezekiel's nose and driving the bone up into his brain. "Die, shit-eater," God hisses under his breath. Ezekiel's body stands motionless for a moment, then suddenly starts to hump the air (sickeningly, it happens every time), then stops, teeters for a beat, and falls flat onto its back, its stiff little erection popping straight up. God grabs Ezekiel by the hair and twists his neck roughly until the head pops off, then roughly throws the head down a trash chute. But it's pointless and God knows it. It doesn't matter what he does anymore; it won't be long before Ezekiel's back again.

A moment later, God collapses heavily into his throne. A long moment of silence and stillness passes. Then a soft voice begins to murmur in God's ear. *"You are wonderful, Lord,"* the voice purrs. *"You are perfect."* It is God's talking throne. Originally, the throne had merely "rumbled" (NT Rev. 4:5), but God had quickly trained it to speak in full sentences: i.e., *"You are excellent, Lord, you are beloved, you are worshipped by all, etc., etc., etc."* The throne was *correct* in all of these statements, obviously. But still— God had by this time come to hate it. Once God had tried to "kill" the throne, but when he hit it with a sledgehammer, it shrieked like an old woman, so he stopped and never tried to kill it again. It *was* still his best and most comfortable chair and he didn't actually want to destroy it, so he let it be, the price being that it would occasionally not stop talking. *"You are marvelous, God,"* the throne murmurs. *"You are omni-benevolent."* Once God had adored this word; it had made him feel, well, honestly, *tingly* all over. At one point, in fact, during a particularly difficult stretch with mankind, God had actually started writing "affirmations" to himself and "I am omni-benevolent" had been his very favorite one. Now, however, he finds that he despises the word.

"Everyone respects you, Lord," the throne coos.

God's jaw tightens.

"Everyone worships you."

"Shut up," God whispers.

"*Everyone loves you.*"

"Shut up, shut up, SHUT UP!!"

"*And that is because you are PURE GOOD.*"

"SHHUUUUUTTTTTTUUUUUUPPPPPPPP!!"

God's voice echoes through the empty palace for a moment— then everything is silent once again and God stares forward at nothing in particular.

CHAPTER ELEVEN

Around the year 350, God hit on a *spectacular* idea. "I will write a *new book*," he suddenly cried out. "Describing what *really* happened with Jesus, setting the whole story straight!" Filled with excitement, God charged into his palace and wrote furiously for several years, "on fire," in his own words. After this new book, the Koran, had been completed, God took his time finding the exact right person to recite it to. ("Because there aren't a lot of Abrahams, Moseses or Solomons in the world, you know what I'm saying, Gabriel?")

In the 400s, God took a brief liking to a man named Augustine. He had loved Augustine's description of human life as "hell on Earth." "Exactly right," God had nodded to himself. What God had been *less* happy with was the way Augustine had turned seemingly everything into some sort of an allegory about Jesus' life. "The ram that Abraham sacrificed did *not* symbolize Jesus, and creating Eve was definitely not a 'prophecy' about him! Sometimes I just *did* things, okay, Augustine?!" Also, to be blunt, God had been offended by the way Augustine had talked about what he described as "musical farts." "That is a grotesque oxymoron!" God had barked. "Farts are not 'musical' in any way;

they are disgusting, just like everything else that pertains to the human body!" Also, when you got right down to it, Augustine had pretty much stolen the idea of God's infinite perfection from Plato (who was, by the way, *far* too gay for God, overall.)

Then, finally, around the year 630, God found his new prophet and, oh my goodness, what a man he was! Muhammad was tall and powerfully built, a brilliant thinker and a fierce warrior. "Not scared to break a few eggs to make an omelette!" is how God had frequently described him. When God sat Muhammad down and began to present the Koran to him, he was determined from the start to leave *zero* room for misunderstanding. This new book was the Truth, God had quickly informed Muhammad—unambiguous, unquestionable, and absolute. "This is the Book (and God capitalized "Book" to make it obvious to Muhammad just how important it really was) that is free of doubt." (K, 2:1) I mean, fine, God's other, older books had technically been "perfect" too, but they had also been, in hindsight, far too open to interpretation. "I put two different creation stories right at the start of my first book! (OT, Gen. 1:1–2:4 vs 2:5–2:22) There were four different narratives about Jesus in my second book!" "But those old messages are now *cancelled*," God instructed Muhammad. (K, 2:106) "They belong in the trash!"

God had decided that the Koran (or as he liked to call it, "my definitive statement") would be beyond criticism of any kind. Anyone who challenged *this* book would suffer, and badly! As for anyone who had the audacity (or frankly the foolishness) to *mock* this book? They would obviously be an agent of Satan and they would pay dearly for their dark alliance! God had wanted to make it crystal clear at the outset that disbelief—which he *wanted*, quite obviously (K, 5:48; 4:155)—would be punished harshly. "I will threaten punishment on almost every page of the Koran," God had noted approvingly to himself. "*That* will make mankind stop doubting me! (Or it *would*, that is, if I *wanted* them to stop doubting me, which I obviously don't, haha!)"

Regarding the Jews: Yes, God had definitely spoken to them, and yes, they had certainly been his chosen people for a time. But now? They were *disgraceful* (K, 4:46) and God hated them. (Fine, he'd always *basically* hated them, but way more so now. "I'm gonna mess their faces up," God sometimes whispered to himself.) (K, 4:47) As for the Christians? They were even worse than the Jews! Sure, God had spoken to them also, had chosen them to be his people for a while too, but they had proceeded to *completely* misunderstood him! The Christians had *actually* believed that Jesus was God's biological son, which was obviously an absurd idea because of *course* he wasn't, God didn't need a *son,* God didn't need anyone, this whole story was about God and *only* God! "The Jews were wicked and bad, but at least they understood that I was the center of the story, you know what I mean, Gabriel? The Christians, on the other hand (who were *actually* just sort of confused Jews, when you think about it), had one big idea, which turned out to be totally 100% wrong!"

Anyway—whatever confusion had existed up to this point, well, it was about to end. The Koran, at long last, was going to bring all of mankind together. (K, 3:9) That had been a great feeling for God. Of course, those who *didn't* accept the Koran would have to be killed. (K, 2:191) Or at the very least have their feet cut off. (K, 5:33) But whatever.

The most essential thing which God had needed to clarify to Muhammad was that Jesus had not been his son. But God had felt that as long as he and Muhammad were talking, he might as well use their conversations to straighten out some other misunderstandings that had built up over the years. For instance, God now explained to Muhammad *exactly* what had happened at the start of the earth. It had gone like this: First of all, God had mixed semen into dirt. (K, 16:4) This wasn't messy in the least, by the way, and here's why: Because it was only *one single drop* of semen, okay? (Gazing down on all those men who later ejaculated like stallions, God had often thought to himself, "Unnecessary! Overkill!") This sperm-mud blend had then "speed-formed" into what at first had looked like a piece of chewed-up meat (K, 22:5), but had then fairly quickly turned into an adult human male.

God had instantly demanded that his angels (who were all there with him from the start, needless to say, and what's odd about that?) bow down before Adam, but Satan had refused. God got annoyed every single time he recalled their subsequent conversation. "Why won't you bow down to Adam?" God had angrily demanded. (K, 15:27) "How could I bow down before a mortal made of clay dried tingling hard?" Satan had responded. (K, Al 15:33)

God's initial reaction had been to say, "'Tingling hard?' What kind of pretentious description of dried clay is *that*, Satan?" But instead he had thundered, "Descend to Hell, you insolent creature. You are hereby damned!" (Q: Why had God invariably capitalized the word "Hell" in the Koran? Answer: Uhh . . . Maybe because it had been the *point* of the whole thing?)

"Can my damnation wait until the raising of the dead?" Satan had quickly asked (K, 15:36), and God remembered thinking at the time, "The raising of the dead won't happen until Judgment Day, which is a *long* ways off, like at the very end of this whole story, in fact! I think that is an incredibly unreasonable request, but you know what, I will instantly agree to it." "Yes," God had quickly responded to Satan, "that is okay with me." That *should* have been the end of their little dustup . . . but then Satan had started harassing God! "Since you tricked me into error," Satan had said (which was absolutely true, God *had* tricked Satan into error; he wasn't quite sure *how* he had done it, but he knew he definitely had), "I will trick your humans."

"Begone, devil!" God had then yelled at Satan. ("I just said *yes* to your highly unreasonable request and now you're giving me grief like this?" is what he was thinking.) "You are contemptible," God had snarled as he sent Satan tumbling down to Hell. "Anyone who listens to you—which, to reiterate, I will *want* them to do, which I will *tempt* them into doing—(K, 6:123) but still, anyone who does so will follow you straight into Hell!" (A question had crossed God's mind at that point: Wouldn't it have made more sense for Satan to tempt *good* people? What exactly was the point of him luring bad people into being bad? Wasn't it somewhat like making sure that 2+2=4? But this was a ridiculous question and therefore easily refuted: If God had wanted 2+2 to equal 5 it definitely would have!)

"*Still* can't believe how quickly Satan got Adam and Eve to strip!" God mutters to himself, slumped in his talking throne. (K, 7:27) God had created Adam and Eve fully dressed, obviously. Human bodies, God had felt from the start, were vile, hideous things. They should be covered up as much as possible. God had actually begun to wish by this time that he'd clothed animals. He abhorred the sight of swollen monkey bottoms and dangling donkey penises. Next time around, he'd give the humans a new commandment: "Dress ye all animals so that their nakedness will not offend the Lord, your God. (Ye may leave fish and insects nude but birds must be clothed, including bat-birds.")

CHAPTER TWELVE

Another thing God had taken this opportunity to clear up with Muhammad: When Cain and Abel had had their battle over which one of them God liked better (it was Abel needless to say because he brought barbecue while Cain brought a bunch of boring vegetables), Cain had looked at his brother and said, "I will murder you," and Abel (who was nude, by the way), had responded with a rather lengthy speech, the central point of which was, "Because I fear God, I will not fight you, I'd rather *you* suffer his punishment and become an inmate of Hell." (K, 5:27–29) Cain then killed Abel and indeed gone to Hell for it. (Cain had in fact been the *first* person to be sent to Hell. "Most people didn't even know Hell *existed* back then," God later mused. "They foolishly believed in a place called 'sheol,' which it turns out was completely made up! How funny.") After Cain had killed Abel, God sent a raven down to scratch a diagram in the dirt demonstrating to Cain how to cover his dead brother's penis and balls. (K, 5:27–31) "I'm still not quite sure why Abel was nude," God had thought. "I *think* he stripped while he was making that pretentious speech but I don't know. I'm also not sure why I had to send a raven down with directions regarding how to cover a penis and balls because, I mean, it's kind of self-explanatory, right?"

Yet another clarification God had wanted to make to Muhammad: When Noah's wife had died, God wanted it to be understood that he had immediately sent her to Hell. (K, 21:10) "First of all, I don't think she believed in Noah," God had explained to Gabriel at the time. Even as the whole earth was flooded, exactly as Noah had predicted, she had *still* doubted him. (Which was, when you thought about it, kind of moronic, because there hadn't been much to *doubt* at that point, but whatever, she still had.) God had also been pretty sure that Noah's wife had cheated on her husband with one of their sons, most likely that evil, penis-gazing youngest one, Ham. (OT, Gen. 9:22–25)

Lot's wife was roasting in Hell too, God had informed Muhammad. Why? Because she had openly disobeyed one of his angels, that's why! "Don't look back," the angel had commanded her and really, can you be any clearer than *that*? But the old hag had looked back, so God, enraged, had instantly turned her into a salt-statue and then sent her plunging to Hell. So what if she had been married to a pervert who mainly wanted to have sex with their daughters or volunteer them for a gangbang? "Taste the eternal flames of punishment, old woman!" God had bellowed. (Because Lot's wife had *definitely* looked like an old woman [K, 26:171] and God had found that repulsive. Old men? The very best thing to be. Old women? Abominations.) As Lot's wife plummeted downward, shrieking in terror, God had called after her "*No one* escapes my perfect justice, you horrid old salt-crone! NO ONE! In the end, *everyone is punished*." (And because God had known that was true, it had sent a shiver of . . . what was it? . . . excitement? . . . dread? . . . straight through him.)

One final clarification: God had long been disgruntled with the way Solomon had portrayed him in the Book of Job, so he used this opportunity to explain to Muhammad what had *actually* happened back then. When Job had cried out to God that he was in physical agony, God had *instantly* relieved him. (K, 21:83–84) "I told him to sit in cold water and rub herbs on himself and after that he felt much better." (K, 38:41) Why hadn't Solomon talked about THAT? It was galling, and not only because God had given Solomon all that great wisdom but additionally because he now remembered that he'd also given him the ability to talk to birds as well as to control genies! (K, 27:16–22) "Damned Jewish ingrate," God had muttered to himself. "Makes me *glad* I gave him that pinkie-dick." (OT, 1K 12:10) But God had gotten Solomon back in the end. He'd had him die standing up, then had weevils eat the walking stick out from underneath him so that his corpse suddenly toppled to the ground. (K, 34:14) "*That* was hilarious," God chuckles thickly to himself, half-slumped over in his throne.

But of course, the *main* thing that God had needed to clear up in the Koran, kind of the whole point of the book in a way, was to tell Muhammad that Jesus had *not* been his son, that he had merely been a human being. A very *illustrious* human being, yes, admittedly, but definitely *not* God's son. "The truth was, it would have been beneath my *glory* to father a son, okay?" God later told Gabriel. (K, 4:171) "I was simply too *immaculate* for that." (K, 19:35) With regard to the question "Who *was* Jesus' father?" the correct answer was: No one. Jesus had *no* father. When Mary got pregnant, there had been no sperm involved at all, just a kind of, oh, call it "magic breath," if you like. (K, 21:91)

While Mary was giving birth to Jesus—by herself under a palm tree, *obviously* (K, 19:18)—she had cried out in pain, so God had instantly had an angel (whom he had thoughtfully prestationed beneath the ground) call up to her: "God has provided dates for you, shake the tree and they will fall." Mary shook the tree and the dates fell and she ate them and felt much better, and God remembered puffing up with pride about that. (K, 19:23–25)

When Mary brought normal-human-baby Jesus out for people to meet, something surprising happened. The baby suddenly made an announcement to them all: "I am a servant of God," the baby began. "He has given me a Book and made me a prophet and blessed me wherever I may be for as long as I live." People stood there in stunned silence as week-old baby Jesus continued to lecture them. "There was peace on the day I was born and there will be peace on the day I die and also on the day I am raised from the dead," the baby proclaimed. (K, 19:30–33) "Why did I wait until Jesus was thirty for him to begin his preaching?" God remembered asking himself. "Why did I not let the talking baby start preaching right then? That would have been *amazing*, right? A talking baby—that would've been like the greatest circus act of all time! That would have done the trick!"

But that had instantly been followed by "Do *what* trick? What am I even trying to accomplish here? If Jesus was a normal human baby, then why did I just have him predict his own death and resurrection?"

This question had seemed thorny for a moment, but the answer quickly became obvious: The baby had lied. The truth was that he *wasn't* going to "die." Here's what was actually going to happen: When things got hot for Jesus, God was going to fly him up to heaven and have a *look-alike* get crucified. (K, 4:157) ("Sort of like when that look-alike replaced Paul McCartney after he was beheaded in that car accident," God much later reflected to himself. God was one of the very few people who preferred Wings to the Beatles, by the way. The main reason for that was that he abhorred John Lennon. "Oh, I'm a 'concept,' am I?!") "I will not die on the cross," the baby should have said, if it was going to be completely truthful. "My *look-alike* will die. Therefore, because I will not actually *be* dead, I could not possibly be 'raised from the dead.'"

When Jesus had first arrived in heaven after God yanked him out of the trouble he was in and replaced him with that unfortunate look-alike, God had prepared a beautiful speech for the moment. (K, 5:110–120) "Oh Jesus, son of Mary," God began, "Remember how good I have been to you and your mother, Mary. Remember how I made you a talking baby. Remember how I let you heal people and raise the dead and also how I made people *not* believe in you and accuse you of magic?"

Jesus just stood there and stared at God, inscrutable as always. God continued, now raising his voice a little bit. "Remember when your followers asked for food, Jesus, and you told them to believe in me and they said 'food will make us believe in God,' so you asked me to send down food because I was the best giver of food (which was true, obviously, and I thank you for pointing it out) and remember how I said 'I *will* send down food, but if anyone disbelieves in me after *this*, I will most definitely hurt them?'"

Jesus still just stood there, staring silently back at God. God rolled on, not liking how shrill his voice was starting to sound now. ("I'm talking too much and that's never ever a good thing," had crossed his mind.) "Did you tell people, 'My mother and I are *gods*,' Jesus?" God demanded, before instantly answering his own question. "No, you did *not*. You told them to worship only me, Jesus. You told them that I was powerful, mighty, and wise and that they should subject themselves to my always-just punishment and that the only true happiness lay in obeying ME because I control everything in every single way! Do you remember that conversation, Jesus, *do you*?"

Jesus stared at God for a long moment, then slowly dropped his head and looked at the ground. "He doesn't seem to remember," God thought to himself. "That's strange. How can he not remember?"

"*Because it never happened perhaps?*"

"SILENCE, DOUBT!"

CHAPTER THIRTEEN

Eventually, God had gotten so sick of doubters ("there's only *this* world," *that* asinine argument; how infuriating of people to not believe in God's glorious, invisible world!) that he had basically turned a bunch of them into moldy garbage. (K, 23:41) The hardest part about doing this had not been, as you might guess, turning people into garbage, but rather instantly making the garbage *moldy.* "Mold grows so *slowly!*" God had muttered angrily, staring down at the non-moldy garbage for hours before finally using all of his powers to speed-grow mold on it. After God had turned the doubters into moldy garbage, he then shoved them face-first into Hell, and do you know why? Because they were *insane,* that's why. (K, 54:47) Even if these insane sinners had *repented,* God *still* wouldn't have forgiven them! (K, 3:90) Here's what he would have done instead: Turn the flames up on them! (K, 17:97)

Some doubters had actually had the gall to *laugh* at Muhammad. (K, 25:41; 45:9) That had incensed God in a way that literally nothing else ever had (which was saying *a lot,* granted, because God was incensed most of the time, but still, it's true.) There was something about laughter that felt terribly corrosive to God; it suggested a lack of respect, obviously, but more than that a lack of *fear*. God wanted humans to be scared of him and he felt that laughter undermined fear completely and therefore he always despised it.

The truth was, even those who *didn't* doubt Muhammad had become annoying to God by this time. First off, there was the way Muhammad's followers had prayed: All too often, drunk, sexually aroused, or, worst of all, needing to take a dump. God would have none of those things. "I want you to be *clean* when you pray to me," he instructed his people. "If you can't find water, don't worry about that part, take a dirt-bath, that'll be fine; I'm perfectly okay with dirt-baths. (K, 4:43) Just make sure you don't pray to me when you're drunk, aroused, or needing to take a dump, is that *clear?*" Then there was the annoying way the prophet's followers would sometimes stroll into his house uninvited and demand, "When's dinner, Muhammad?" (K, 33:53) God had disliked that intensely. "*Only* go to the prophet's house when you're *invited*, only at the set time, and then leave promptly after you're finished," God commanded his people. "Stop inconveniencing my prophet!" (There had undeniably been moments when God was struck by how relatively *trivial* his concerns could seem. "I created the entire universe and now I'm giving people instructions regarding dinner manners? That seems, I don't know . . . incongruous?")

Knowing beforehand that Muhammad was going to have to deal with a whole lot of irritating people, God created some excellent comebacks for him to use against them. God had worked on these put-downs for quite a while during the writing of the Koran, because he had wanted them to be as devastating as possible. "*Wish for death if what you say is true*" had been a splendid one, God felt. (K, 2:93) He had liked it so much, in fact, that it actually became his unofficial "catchphrase" for several years. He had even made a T-shirt with that line printed on it.

Another comeback God had been proud of was *"Now taste the agony of burning!"* (K, 3:181) This one sounded especially scary when you emphasized the word "burning." "Now taste the agony of BURNING!" God had repeated it to himself over and over, loving it every single time. It sounded *slightly* less scary when you stressed "agony." "Now taste the AGONY of burning!" Emphasizing "taste" was even less scary. "Now TASTE the agony of burning!" And stressing the other words obviously wasn't scary in the least: "Now taste THE agony OF burning?" ("Articles and prepositions are not scary, *period!*")

Another line God had quite enjoyed, and this one was meant to be said in a quiet but chilling little voice, *just* above a whisper and therefore super intimidating: *"Taste the torment of the fire which you used to deny."* (K, 34:42) Much later, during the period that was called "Judgment Day" (which, to jump ahead for a moment, had turned out to be a *serious* misnomer; it took a *lot* longer than one day to bring all those dead people back to life and then send them tumbling down to Hell. "Judgment Day" had turned out to be more like "Judgment *Decade*," if you really want to know the truth), God used *"Taste the torment of the fire which you used to deny"* a great deal and it had felt marvelous every single time.

Yet another one of God's favorite lines had been *"Enter then the fire!"* (K, 7:38) To add extra "pop" to this one (not that it *needed* extra pop, obviously it didn't, but still), God then cried out *"With the genies!"* God had definitely regretted creating genies by this point. He had, in fact, decided to end the entire Koran with a rather blunt warning to Muhammad: *"Beware of genies."* (K, 114:6) (Not that it matters, but God had also come to hate monkeys. "Monkeys are *despicable*," he had announced loudly. [K, 5:60] "I loathe the way they jump around and make faces and screech, like they think they are 'cute' or something. They are *not* cute, they are vile little abominations.")

One put-down line that God had ended up feeling slightly ambivalent about was "*Enter the gates of Hell and live there forever.*" (K, 16:29) Or rather, that *first* part he had liked just fine, but what came after it hadn't felt quite as good: "*How dreadful a dwelling for the haughty.*" "Using 'dreadful' and 'haughty' in the same sentence doesn't make me sound tough," God had thought to himself. "It makes me sound like a pompous a-hole!"

CHAPTER FOURTEEN

At a certain point in the writing of the Koran, God had started to wonder if maybe he was *slightly* overdoing it on the punishment side of things. "Maybe it'd be a good idea to talk a little bit more about the *reward* side," he thought. God decided to describe to Muhammad what *good* people could expect at the end of their lives (other than the unspeakable joy of knowing that everyone else was burning, eating cactus, and drinking boiling water, haha!) (K, 35:36–37) Granted, there wouldn't be very *many* good people in the end, hardly any really, like one tenth of one percent of mankind maybe, but still, for that tiny little minority of human beings that never *ever* doubted God's perfection (and God frankly doubted whether such people even existed), for them there would be Paradise.

Life in Paradise would be marvelous, God informed Muhammad. People would wear lots of jewelry; their clothes would be silk and they would lounge around on couches and carpets, murmuring "Peace, peace" to each other (K, 35:33) while sipping sparkling wine (K, 47:15)—nonalcoholic needless to say! (K, 37:47) There would also be (and this is where God had surprised himself, at least at first) big-eyed virgins (K,

37:48; 55:56), lovely young maidens who had never been with either man or genie. (Women who'd had sex with genies were extremely slutty, in God's opinion. "Why would anyone sleep with a *genie*?" he had repeatedly demanded.) These virginal young maidens would be available to the men in Paradise for eternal lovemaking, God informed Muhammad. (Q: Would the lovemaking be procreative? A: No, obviously not. God didn't want a bunch of screaming babies in Paradise. The maidens would have to be "fixed" so that they could never get pregnant.)

God remembered stopping at that point and mulling over what he had just written, feeling frankly confused by it. "This makes no *sense*," he thought to himself. "I hate sex, I always have. Why would I want it in *Paradise*?"

Then, in a flash, God understood. "Of *course*," he exclaimed with a broad smile. "The virgins are a *temptation*." He decided to go one step further: "I will also surround those few good men in Paradise with handsome lads!" (K, 76:19) "Only the ones who *decline* to have sex with these nubile youths will get to *stay* in Paradise," he mused. God loved to imagine a man who'd comported himself perfectly in life and had just arrived in Paradise. There he sat, reclining on a couch in his brocaded silk robe, sporting a chunky silver bracelet and drinking nonalcoholic wine and feeling pretty damned great about himself—until he looked at one of those perfectly formed boys and thought to himself, "*At last, my eternal reward*," but the moment he touched one of those eternally firm buttocks, guess what, he would find himself plunging straight to Hell! "If *anyone* thinks there's going to be homosexual hanky-panky going on in Paradise, they've got another thing coming!!" God had yelled loudly to no one in particular.

And if you're wondering whether maybe those beautiful boys would be in Paradise to tempt the *ladies*, well, the answer to that is no and here's why: Because there weren't going to *be* any ladies in Paradise! "Who would it be?" God had sometimes demanded of Gabriel. "I mean, seriously, *who*? Eve, who instantly disobeyed me? Sarah, who laughed at me? Mary, who doubted me? Lot's wife? Noah's wife? Honestly—who?!" The truth was, God had informed Muhammad, that women were like fields— meant to be plowed. (K, 2:223) Thinking back five hundred-plus years, God realized that Paul had been absolutely correct when he'd said that women were literally *incapable* of understanding truth. (NT, 2 Tim. 3:7) "And *that* is why I told Luke that only *men* were holy!" God crowed proudly. (NT, Lu. 2:23)

(Eventually, God decided that he might allow one girl into Paradise: Jephthah's daughter. It's not that he felt "guilty" about what had happened to the girl, obviously; he did not. [OT, Jud. 11:31–39] A deal was a deal, after all, and the girl needed to be killed in order for her father to defeat the Ammonites. Still, God couldn't deny that at certain moments, thinking back on watching Jephthah murder his poor crying daughter—yes, it did bother him. "I will allow Jephthah's daughter into Paradise!" God had suddenly announced one day. "Why, I might even learn her name at some point!" [OT, Jud. 11:40])

(As for those eternal sex-bots or whatever you wanted to call them, as soon as God was done with them, he'd destroyed them. He certainly wasn't going to allow them to drift off and start having sex with genies. He'd dashed their brains—which were tiny anyway, what did they need brains for?—out on rocks.)

Near the end of the Koran, God began to have some very puzzling second thoughts about—well, basically everything he'd just written. The Jews and the Christians *were* completely wrong about things, he had told Muhammad, but still . . . didn't they believe in the most important thing of all, Him? Did he genuinely want them punished for all eternity? Nonbelievers, yes, definitely, they were beyond any hope. But other God- believers? Weren't they, in some sense, the *best* of his created beings? (K, 98:7–8) Mightn't they go to Paradise too and live there forever?

Then God had found himself softening even more. Even to those who *didn't* believe in him, why not just say, "You go your way and I'll go mine?" he asked. (K, 109:6) Why did people have to fight about this stuff? So they *disagreed* about things, what was so terrible about that? They could think different things, even *pray* to different gods, and leave each other alone. "Why can't you all just be *kind* to each other?" God asked mankind. (K, 90:17)

And with that (as well as a few *brief* threats against one particular man and his wife; the man would have to be burned, the wife would have to be hung) (K, 111:1–5), God was done.

"I will never have to speak to mankind again," he thought to himself at that moment with supreme satisfaction. "That is wonderful."

He experienced a brief moment of blissful calm. Then, grotesquely, that devilish inner voice whispered to God.

"*Are you sure?*"

"*Be silent!*" God instantly responded.

"*Who says they are free of doubt except the man who is plagued with it?*"

"*ENOUGH!*"

"*Who forbids questions except the man who is terrified of them?*"

"SILENCE DOUBT!"

But doubt, it was by now rather obvious, could not be, could never be, completely silenced.

CHAPTER FIFTEEN

Over the next thousand-plus years, as God watched the followers of his various prophets fighting and killing each other, he couldn't help but occasionally wonder: "What am I doing *wrong* here? I tried to clarify things with the Koran, to set everything straight, but I only seem to have muddied things up more by adding different versions of the exact same stories. How are the humans supposed to know which story is *actually* true at this point? Is it the older version, told closer to the events described? Or the newer version, told with presumably more perspective?" While it was undeniably the case that the Koran had worked in some parts of the world—there were people who *loved* it—it was equally true that many other people seemed unconvinced. "The Jews don't believe it, the Christians don't believe it, the Asians . . . well, who cares about the Asians?"

"What are people saying about me?" God sometimes demanded of Gabriel during this long, confusing stretch of time. What he heard back was, frankly, a mixed bag. On the one hand, God had *adored* John Calvin. "Now *that* is a man who understands me," he cried out upon first hearing Calvin's words. "Human beings *ARE* rotten, evil worms and the only thing they need to understand is their utter NOTHINGNESS, exactly, *exactly*!" Even babies, as Calvin had pointed out, were wicked. Why? Because they were created carnally, which was vile to start with (the *best* life for humans, as Calvin had made clear, involved zero sex; the *luckiest* humans, in fact, were those whom God had instructed to cut their balls off!), but beyond that, babies were little seedbeds of sin, and therefore odious to God. "Evil before they were even *born*, pathetic," God had murmured to himself. Another thing Calvin had nailed was that God only loved *some* people. Why? "Because it would have been *promiscuous* for me to love everyone! Also, guess what, I don't love everyone because I don't want to!" (One thing God *hadn't* appreciated was the way Calvin had described Satan as both "daring" and "powerful." "Wrong!" God had instantly rejoindered. "Satan was weak and cowardly, exactly as I made him so that he could foil me at every turn!")

On the other hand, God had found Rene Descartes' notion of an all-powerful and all-knowing *demon* who was constantly tricking mankind bothersome. Where exactly had he come up with *that* crazy idea? As for Baruch Spinoza's whole "I don't differentiate between God and nature" argument? Well, that was absolutely unacceptable; God had made it clear a long time earlier that anyone who worshipped nature should be killed. (OT, Deut. 17:3) Regarding Blaise Pascal's so-called wager vis-à-vis God's existence, well, the less said about that one the better. "I don't want humans believing in me simply so they can win a bet and go to heaven! Anyone who does that—and believe me, I will *know*—will definitely burn." God also didn't think much of Anselm's so-called "ontological" argument for his existence. "You can't simply *define* me into existence, Anselm!" As for Thomas Aquinas, God had never been able to get through him without falling asleep.

But the thinker who had *really* gotten under God's skin was David Hume. "This obese prick is *openly mocking* me," God had gasped when he first read Hume's *Dialogues Concerning Natural Religion*. In this monstrous book, Hume had had the temerity to suggest that God was senile—ineffective—a child—even a *vegetable*. "I am NOT a vegetable!" God had yelled loudly when he read this, and everyone present in heaven had shaken their heads and clucked disapprovingly. How *dare* Hume imply that God was a vegetable?! Less than two hundred years earlier, God had made sure that Giordano Bruno was burned at the stake for having the nerve to suggest that the universe was vast, possibly even infinite, and that there might actually be life elsewhere. "WRONG!" God had shouted at the time. "WRONG WRONG WRONG! The universe is NOT infinite, the stars are NOT other suns and there is no other life ANYWHERE but Earth and even if there is I don't want to HEAR about it, now BURN BRUNO!" And they had too. That's how things had been back in what God had semi-facetiously come to call the "good ol' days." (It was semi-facetious, obviously, because there *were* no good ol' days, they'd all been bad, just in different ways.)

But David Hume had not been burned, nor had he been stoned or impaled or stomped on by horses or eaten by dogs and pooped out or anything else. No, David Hume had gotten away with his hideous insults to God. Fine, Immanuel Kant had *responded* to him, but it was such a *feeble* defense. "Hume can't *prove* that I don't exist? That's the best you can do, Kant?!" Søren Kierkegaard's later defense of God was even worse! "People should believe in me because it makes no *sense* to do so? Am I supposed to feel good about that, Kierkegaard?" (As for the thinker who would later call himself the "Antichrist," the one who would say that God was dead, well, God hated him the most of all. "Burn in hell, you syphilitic madman," God would sometimes curse under his breath.) In the Islamic world, God had felt, David Hume would have been butchered for what he had said. "*Those* folks still know how to get it done!" he had noted approvingly at the time. ("But will they *still* in the year

2400 when *their* religion is eighteen hundred years old?" God had wondered, honestly doubting it. "They'll probably turn all namby-pamby, just like everyone else.")

But as annoying as the Hume thing had been, there had been a far deeper problem growing. As centuries had passed, God had grown increasingly uncomfortable with what he had told Muhammad about Jesus. Now it's true, Jesus had been presumptuous and self-obsessed during his time on Earth, and he *had* gotten under God's skin with some of the things he'd said and done. Because of that, in what he now regarded as a fit of pique, God had told Muhammad that Jesus was not his son. But Jesus *was* his son, God knew that now. ("How do I know? Because no one else's death ever affected me the way his did. Also, if he *wasn't* my son, why would I have created so many knockoff versions of him? There was no 'Swordmouth Moses' or 'Lamb David' or 'Baby Muhammad,' you know what I mean, Gabriel?") "I had my son tortured to death, then wrote an entire book denying he was my son," God found himself thinking. "I kind of need to fix this. But *how?*"

Right around that time, a young man named Joseph Smith had gazed up at heaven and asked plaintively: "Which religion is *true*, Lord?" God didn't respond to everyone who asked him such questions obviously. "I'd never have time to do anything else if I did!" he had observed dryly, but young Smith's timing had turned out to be extremely fortuitous. "That is the *exact* question I need to answer," God thought to himself. (Smith was a magnificent young fellow, by the way—strapping, handsome, charming, "another Muhammad," in God's words. "It's fascinating how I always pick such powerfully charismatic men," God once noted to himself. "I suppose it's because if I didn't, no one would believe—wait, that's not right.")

"But what will I *tell* young Smith?" God asked himself. "What I really *need* is another *book*—but do I have one ready?"

God hesitated for a long moment at that point, thinking things over, stroking his beard thoughtfully—before suddenly sitting bolt upright. "Wait a minute," he thought. "*Wait a minute. Is it* possible that I *already* wrote the next book? . . . My god, I think it *is* . . . I *know* it is, in fact! This is *amazing.* Somehow, over 2,400 years ago, *foreseeing that this exact moment would arrive, I specifically prepared for it with what I already know will be my greatest book, the one that will finally tell my TRUE story and therefore make all of mankind UNDERSTAND me!*"

CHAPTER SIXTEEN

The Book of Mormon had begun simply. Back in the year 600 BC, knowing that the Temple in Jerusalem was about to fall, God had sent an angel down to speak to a man named Lehi. The angel had told Lehi to escape this upcoming disaster by traveling to North America and essentially starting an entire new civilization there. (BOM, 1N 1:1) Lehi had warned his fellow Jews about what was going to happen, but had they listened to him? No, of course they hadn't; they had wickedly mocked him, those damned Jews. (BOM 1N 1:19) God had then allowed Lehi to sort of "vision-visit" heaven and observe him sitting on his almighty throne surrounded by angels singing his praises. (BOM, 1N 1:8) After that, Jesus had flown down to Earth, handed Lehi a book, and told him to read it. (BOM, 1N 1:11) "I'm not *totally* sure what the book was," God had thought later. "But I *think* it was the Book of Mormon, which apparently already existed." Lehi read the book, then looked at God and complimented his throne. (BOM, 1N 1:14) Which had been utterly unnecessary, needless to say, because God had already *known* that his throne was in heaven. He didn't need some guy to tell him that.

God recalled the strained conversation he'd had with Jesus in heaven around this time. "Why not send me down to earth *now*, Father?" Jesus had asked him.

God had shaken his head firmly. "Definitely not, Jesus, *definitely* not."

"But people already *know* I'm coming, Father. The Book of Mormon tells them *everything* about me, long before I even show up. Literally *nothing* about me will be a surprise to them. (BOM, 1N 11:27–36) Why not let me fly down to North America and start talking to people right now, get them off to a good start? After that I could travel through South America . . ."

"I don't give a damn about South America, Jesus!"

". . . Then cross the Pacific to Asia."

"I *definitely* don't give a damn about Asia! Have I not made that clear? Why do you think I told Paul 'Don't go to Asia,' eh?" (NT, Acts 16:6)

"Fine. Then I could, however you want to put it, 'return' to the Middle East."

"The one part of the world I DO care about!"

"And my point is I could get there six hundred years earlier, Father."

"As I said, I don't like it, Jesus."

"But *why*?"

"For one thing, you need to be born to a human woman, alright?"

"But I already exist, Father, I'm here. What possible purpose is served by me waiting six hundred years to be born to a human mother? Will I learn something from her?"

"Certainly not, you will be exactly as you are now! The truth is, I'm not even sure if Mary's really going to be your 'mother' exactly. She might be more of a *womb* for you to grow inside."

"Fine, then as I said, we don't need to wait. If you think it's *absolutely* necessary for me to be born to a human woman, then why not let me be born to a woman in North America right *now* and start growing into being, well . . . *myself?* We can get things *started* is what I'm saying, Father."

"Well, I'm sorry, but that's simply *not* the plan, Jesus."

"Father—"

"Excuse me, Jesus. No. The *plan* is to wait six hundred years, then send you down to the Middle East where you will live for thirty essentially pointless years before you speak for a little while and then are violently murdered."

"*Father*—"

"*That* is when you will visit North America, Jesus, *not* before. Then, after your brief appearance in North America—where one appearance will more than suffice, by the way, because North America is a very small continent . . ."

"It's actually not, Father."

"Stop interrupting me. You will *then* be flown back up here to heaven before you are flown back down into your dead body in Jerusalem. At that point, you will mill around for somewhere between one day and two months. (And by the way, Jesus, if you're thinking of wearing 'disguises' when you come back [NT, Mat. 27:51], please don't, alright? It'd be ridiculous and also pointless. What would you be worried about anyway, being caught and 'rekilled'?) At *that* time, you will fly back up to heaven and we will begin to prepare for Judgment Day."

"Do you think it's possible that your plan is unnecessarily complicated, Father?"

"No, Jesus, it is *elegant,* just like all of my plans!"

"Because the truth is we could begin Judgment Day right now if we wanted to, Father."

". . . *What's that?!*"

"I said: We could begin Judgment Day *right now.*"

"Wait, you mean, like right now—right now?"

"It's not like mankind hasn't been sufficiently warned, Father."

"You don't seem to be listening to me, Jesus—as I said, there is a PLAN. To be specific: *My plan.*"

"Yes, well, the problem I'm having, Father, is that *I'm* the one who has to wait around six hundred years to be brutally killed."

God and Jesus never talked about Jesus' crackpot notions again. "Begin Judgment Day *now*, what a stupid idea," God had muttered to himself in disbelief.

CHAPTER SEVENTEEN

Full disclosure: There *had* been moments during the translation of the Book of Mormon when God couldn't help but think something along the lines of: "Why is this book so *bad?* My other books all had, you know, *moments.* The Old Testament was lively and exciting, filled with great characters; the New Testament was more intimate, but quite dramatic; the Koran was at times lyrical and poetic. But this Book of Mormon, which I *supposedly* wrote at my peak—well, honestly—what happened to my writing ability? 'They did humble themselves even in the depths of humility?' (BOM, Mos. 21:35) That's *terrible.* 'The words of your seed will shoot out of my mouth onto your seed?' (BOM, 2N 29:2) That's both terrible and *repulsive.* And that *ridiculously* belabored 'vineyard' parable that I spent seven pages hammering into the damned ground? Even as I was *writing* it, I was bored! (BOM, Jac. 5:1–77) And simply admitting how bad the book was? (BOM, Ether 12:23) That didn't exactly fix the problem!"

Another thing that God couldn't help but notice about the Book of Mormon as Smith's translation continued: It was *supposedly* written by dozens of different people over the course of a thousand years, but in fact all of the authors sounded exactly alike! "If you didn't know better, you'd swear that one person (with zero writing ability, by the way) was writing this book," God had noted to Gabriel at the time. In the Old Testament, there were obviously a lot of voices; some of them were great writers (fine, Solomon), while others were terrible (Isaiah), but you'd never think one person wrote the whole thing. ("Even though, in a sense, one person did: *ME,*" God quickly corrected himself.) The New Testament too had clearly been written by a number of different people. ("I wish it hadn't been, I hate the way they contradicted each other," God said. "But there it is.") The Koran had explicitly been written by one person, so that was fine. But *this* book—why did all the characters sound identical? "I'm no expert on writing," God said ("Wait, yes I am actually because, well, I'm an expert on *everything),* but I'm fairly sure that when all the characters sound exactly the same, that's bad writing." (There was *one* thing about the Book of Mormon that God had felt extremely comfortable with: The absence of women from the story. "At last, a book that essentially removes women completely, I love it!")

Getting back to the story, however.

Lehi had had one purely good son, Nephi, and two purely bad ones, Lemuel and Laman. In time, Nephi would lead an entire civilization of excellent, light-skinned people called "Nephites" while Laman would lead an opposing civilization of wicked, dark-skinned people called "Lamanites." It went without saying that the ancient Hebrews had been extremely fair-skinned, by the way. "Like modern-day *Swedes,*" God had often noted appreciatively. "Whiteness is delightsome," God thought on more than one occasion at this time. (BOM, 2N 5:21) (God had loved using the word "delightsome," finding it vastly superior to the boring "delightful." He had loved "delightsome" so much, in fact, that he had started to toy with using other excellent words, like "beautysome," "wondersome" and "amazesome.")

"I will lead you to a land I have prepared for you," God had instructed Nephi. (BOM, 1N 13:15) Which was absolutely true. God had set aside North America for the Nephites a long time before. When dark-skinned people had tried to enter North America 15,000 years earlier, crossing an ice bridge into what would later be called "Alaska," God had had them all eaten by polar bears. "Not for you!" he had cried down at them. If necessary, God had been prepared to build a giant wall to keep these dark-skinned intruders out of his precious North America.

Correction. *No one* had tried to enter North America 15,000 years earlier and here's why: Because the universe was only 6,000 years old, so it wasn't even possible, that's why! The universe was meant to *look* older, yes, but that was only in order to trick people into believing in extremely pernicious ideas like "Evolution." "Mankind *still* doesn't seem to realize how many traps I have set for them," God had noted with satisfaction at the time. "Without misery, there is no me!" he had shouted to no one in particular. (BOM, Al. 2:13)

Laman and Lemuel had been utterly hopeless. Here's an example: God had sent an angel down to tell them to stop hitting Nephi with a stick. (BOM, 1N 3:28–29) "Stop hitting your brother with that stick," the angel had told them. "God has chosen Nephi to rule over you because you are evil." Pretty straightforward instructions, right? But had Laman and Lemuel listened to the angel? No, they had not. The truth was, no matter what God said to these two idiots, they'd reform for a day or two and then instantly turn wicked again. Another example: When God had had Nephi literally shock his two brothers with his Godly power (BOM, 1N 17:54–55), Laman and Lemuel had stood there, shaking for a long moment like guys who'd stuck forks into electrical outlets. When God had finally stopped shaking them, they acted like they'd finally learned their lesson; they were apologetic, they bowed and scraped. But as soon as they got on the boat headed to North America, guess what Laman and Lemuel and their two wives started doing? Singing and dancing! God *despised* singing and dancing! (BOM, 1N 18:9) "Leave it to the professionals on Broadway, amateurs," he had hissed angrily down at the group. ("More and more, I realize that Broadway musicals were the high-water mark of all human civilization," God mutters to himself. "*Les Mis*, so moving, I always feel for that main character, the police officer.")

After that, Laman and Lemuel tied Nephi up, which had caused his "Liahona" to stop working, and they were all just about to drown when God decided to give them a break. Regarding the "Liahona:" Knowing that the Nephites' journey to North America was going to be exceedingly difficult, God had devised a special tool to help them. The Liahona (and yes, God was very proud of the name—"'Liahona' sounds vaguely *Hawaiian,* doesn't it, Gabriel, and that is quite interesting because 'Hawaiian' doesn't even *exist* and won't for another thousand years!") looked like a cross between what would later be called a Magic 8-Ball and "The Ball" from the 1970's cult horror film *Phantasm.* "Follow the directions of the Liahona," God had instructed Lehi. "But remember: It will *only* work if you believe in it!" (BOM, 1N 16:28)

"*An interesting tool that only works when people believe in it,*" that devilish inner voice had whispered.

"STOP."

"*Doubt undoes you.*"

"ENOUGH!"

"*It always has.*"

"SILENCE!"

"*You know the truth.*"

"*SILENCE, DEVIL!!*"

CHAPTER EIGHTEEN

"Did you ever wonder," Satan once asked while he and God were having a conversation about (what else?) hell, "whether Joseph Smith was simply predicting *himself* when the Book of Mormon supposedly predicted him?" (BOM, 2N 3:6–9)

"In that case," God quickly retorted, "young Smith would have been essentially making the whole thing up, now wouldn't he, Satan?"

"More or less, yes."

God smiled thinly; he had been dealing with Satan for a very long time now and was therefore prepared for his adversary's relentless and nasty cynicism. God leveled a cool gaze at Satan and returned, "But why should we stop with the Book of Mormon, eh, Satan?"

"An excellent question."

"Why not say that Muhammad made up the Koran too, hmm?"

"Why not?"

"And the Gospels? Why not say *they* were made up too, right?"

"Again—why not?"

"Oh, this is *fun*, Satan. Let's keep going. Why not say that Moses and David and Solomon and, oh my goodness, *everyone else in all of the books* simply made things up?"

"Alright."

But this is where God finally lowered the boom on his nemesis. "In that case," God said, "we're left with a bunch of made-up stories, in which *you yourself* are nothing but a made-up character, Satan!"

"A very logical conclusion," Satan replied. "As are you, God."

"As am I! Yes, Satan, exactly, we're both made-up characters, presumably created to serve human emotional needs, specifically those pertaining to *fear*, am I right? I'm the 'Great Father in the Sky' who will protect them while you are the 'Eternal Tempter' who can be blamed for all of their transgressions, isn't that right?"

"Perhaps it is."

"The humans would not be *our* puppets in that case, Satan. We would be *theirs!*"

"Exactly so."

"And *that* would explain why I'm so *obsessed* with mankind, wouldn't it, Satan? Because without them, I literally wouldn't even exist!"

"That's true."

"Ohhhhhhh yes, Satan, yes *indeed*, this all makes *perfect* sense."

"I'm glad you think so, God."

At that point, God exploded, suddenly infuriated by the way this conversation had gone. "I *don't* think so, you fool, I'm being *sarcastic!* It doesn't make 'perfect' sense, it doesn't make ANY sense at all! Do you have zero sense of humor, Satan?"

"I'm sometimes amused by you, God."

"Yes, well, and I'm sometimes amused by you too!" God then shook his head disdainfully. "Is that what you *actually* think, Satan, that you and I are 'made-up characters?' Are you really *that* far gone?"

"I find it to be an interesting thought experiment, that's all. But you don't like those very much, do you, God?"

"No, Satan, I do *not* like them and I'll tell you why: Because what possible purpose could a 'thought experiment' have for one who possesses absolute truth?"

"None, apparently."

"Exactly right, *none*." After a tense pause, God said, in his most witheringly disrespectful voice, "Back to work, devil."

"Yes."

"Where were we?"

"I was just asking you, God, since I'm obviously the one who will be roasting people in hell: Will I be burning the Jews?"

God stared at Satan, who had hesitated for a moment, then continued. "Because of the way they disobeyed you and were so lascivious and also because of the way they killed your son?"

God nodded vaguely. "Yes, that's definitely all true . . . Yes . . . Burn them . . . Burn the Jews . . . Definitely."

Satan wrote something down in a small notebook he carried with him, then looked up at God again. "And what about the Christians?"

"The *Christians*? What do you—?"

"If what you said to Muhammad was true and the Christians were all wrong about Jesus . . ." (K, 3:59–63) Satan paused, studied God carefully. "I'm sorry—what you said in the Koran *was* true, wasn't it, God?"

"Of course it was true! *Everything* I say is true, you know that!"

"So that would mean that I should burn the Christians too then?"

". . . Yes. Burn the Christians too."

"And what about the Muslims, God?"

"Fine!" God erupted. "*They're* bad too, *everyone* is bad, and I want them all to burn eternally because they're all just fragments of me and I want them to suffer, is that what you want to hear, Satan?!"

"Only if it's true, God."

God suddenly felt quite sick of this conversation, so he broadly pantomimed a yawn and said, very loudly, "You're booooorrrrriinng, Satan!" That shut Satan up, especially when God started yelling "BOOOOORRRRRIIIIINNNNG! B O O O O O O R R R R R R I I I I I N N N G G ! BOOOOOORRRRIIIIINNNGG!" over everything Satan said until the devil simply turned and walked away.

This interaction was one of the most irritating ones God had ever had with Satan, but for some annoying reason, sort of like when a bad song got stuck in your head ("Africa" by Toto once got stuck in God's head for a decade—which actually *wasn't* a problem at all because "Africa" was a pretty great song), Satan's nasty question—"How do you know you even exist?"— had lodged itself firmly in God's mind. "It's completely absurd," God told Gabriel. "The idea that humans made ME up—well, it makes me laugh. Doesn't it make you laugh, Gabriel?" Gabriel laughed—but not hard enough. In hindsight, that had been the moment God began to stop trusting him.

CHAPTER NINETEEN

Back to the Book of Mormon.

God despised doubt, he always had. But it was strange. No matter what he said or did to vanquish it, doubt always seemed to return, like a dark and noisome fog rolling back in. Around 500 BC, a man named Sherem had showed up in North America and started to say truly appalling things. "You are worshipping a man who won't even live for nearly *five hundred* years," he said, referring to Jesus. "Or, that is, a man whom you *claim* will live in five hundred years, because the truth is you can't possibly *know* that." Show me some *proof*, Sherem had demanded of the Nephites. "Oh, I'll show you some proof alright, Sherem!" God whispered angrily to himself. Not long afterward, Sherem toppled to the ground and was unable to get up. He was kept alive by a sort of ancient "feeding tube" (BOM, Jac. 7:15) for a few days and in that time he renounced everything wicked he'd said and divulged that he'd been tricked by Satan. ("Knew it," God thought.) Then Sherem died. "Now *that's* the way to deal with doubters!" God crowed to his angels afterward. "Make them fall down, keep them alive through force-feeding for a few days, have them denounce themselves, then kill them. *Gorgeous.*"

(One thing that had frankly confused God about the story of Sherem was the ending, however. As Jacob was wrapping up the chapter, he had closed with the word "Adieu." [BOM, Jac. 7:27] Which had made no sense obviously because, well, this was the year 500 BC in North America, so why the hell was Jacob speaking *French*? "Sometimes things happen in my books which make them seem laughably fraudulent," God had noted at the time. "And that is strange because they are NOT laughably fraudulent, obviously, they are absolutely true. But still—'*Adieu*'?")

Sherem's demise, sadly, hadn't put an end to doubt. Around 100 BC, a man named Nehor showed up and started saying even worse things than Sherem had. "Don't be scared," Nehor told people. "Lift up your heads and *rejoice*! God created and will redeem *all* men! In the end we will all live *forever*!" (BOM, Al. 1:4) "Bullshit," God had instantly shouted. "That is complete bullshit. Yes, I created all men and yes, they will all live forever, but guess what, Nehor, most of them will live forever in *hell*. I don't want humans lifting their heads, I want them keeping their heads down and I definitely want them to *stop rejoicing* because I *hate* rejoicing, almost as much as I hate singing and dancing!" "Give Nehor a super-humiliating death," God then yelled down (BOM, Al. 1:15), and his people did exactly that, impaling Nehor, then letting horses stomp on him and dogs eat him and poop him out—so that had been satisfying.

But it had turned out that Sherem and Nehor were only previews of someone a *lot* worse.

Around a hundred years before Jesus was scheduled to fly down to North America, Satan had done something which God had found utterly shocking: He had created the Antichrist! "What the hell does Satan think he's *doing*?" God had roared when he heard about it. "The Antichrist isn't supposed to appear until the *very end* of this story, when he's supposed to be a giant multiheaded dragon-bear of some kind! (NT, Rev. 13:1–2) Why is Satan sending the Antichrist to earth *now*? And why in the guise of a *man*?"

When this Antichrist, Korihor (or "Kori-whore," as God generally called him), started to preach, well, God found the questions he raised to be old news. "'Why are you waiting for Jesus to arrive? You can't *possibly* know that he's coming blah blah blah'—same old specious nonsense," thought God. Korihor's remarks bugged God, definitely, but what had been genuinely enraging was that they had *worked*. People had instantly fallen for Korihor's message and that had led to—what else?—*whoring*. "Why do humans love to *whore* so damned much?" God had demanded of a nearby angel, who had shrugged so feebly that God had instantly ripped his face off.

"Your traditions are foolish," Korihor had instructed God's people. (BOM, Al. 30:14–28) "Their *actual* purpose is to keep you ignorant and frightened. Priests tell you that you are all guilty because of what Adam did. They like it when your heads are down, they don't *want* you to look up with courage and grasp your basic human rights." Then Korihor's vile message got even worse—*much* worse, in fact. "Priests want you to be scared of offending this made-up being called 'God,' who never has been and never will be either seen or known!" God stared down at Korihor at that moment, heart racing. "Why am I letting him say all these things?" he wondered, on some level genuinely dumbstruck that a moment of such raw power was appearing in this profoundly worthless book. ("You would have to be a monumental ignoramus to believe the Book of Mormon," had by now crossed God's mind on numerous occasions.)

God's man Alma had quickly let the Antichrist have it with a shot of pure, irrefutable logic: "You deny there is a God, Korihor, but behold, I say unto you that I *know* there is a God!" he said. (BOM, Al. 30:39) "Excellent argument, Alma!" God cried down excitedly. "Can you *prove* there is no God?" Alma then demanded of Korihor, and God hooted down derisively, "Can't prove a negative, can you, 'whore'?" Then Alma bored in even further. "You believe as you do, Korihor, because you are possessed by Satan, who is using you to destroy mankind." Now fine, given that Korihor had technically been the "Antichrist," this wasn't *that* deep of an insight on Alma's part, but God still liked the way Alma had articulated it. He had especially liked hearing Satan described as a "lying spirit," because when you got right down to it, lying *was* pretty much all Satan ever did. "I tell the truth and he lies, end of story," God had noted internally. It had made him think of the ancient Greek philosopher Heraclitus' famous line: "Character is destiny." "Absolutely correct," God had thought to himself, "Character IS destiny and it always will be." (As for Heraclitus' *other* big idea, that "you can't step in the same river twice," that is, that change is constant, well that one was completely false. "I NEVER change," God often boasted. "That is what makes me so perfect!")

Korihor then started to argue with Alma but God had instantly yelled, "I don't want to hear any more out of this guy!" and struck Korihor dumb. Oh, *that* had changed his mind, and quick! Now Korihor suddenly believed in God. "I DO believe," he wrote. "In fact, I *always* believed, I was merely being tricked by Satan." ("*Knew* it," God thought to himself.) Then came the question that God always found enjoyable: "How shall I kill this asshole?" When God thought of the answer, he literally laughed out loud. "I will have people stomp him to death!" God had cried in delight. "Stomp on this puppety piece of trash until he's pulp!" Some people called Zoramites did just that and it was glorious to behold! (BOM, Al. 30:59) "The Antichrist got *stomped* to death," God chuckles to himself, shifting heavily in his talking throne. "I *love* that."

CHAPTER TWENTY

As the centuries rolled by, there had definitely been times when God gazed down on the Nephites and Lamanites battling each other and wished that he'd created a few more tribes. North America had turned out to be a very large continent; it could have easily supported lots of tribes, God now understood. It didn't actually have to be just two. There had even been moments when God had looked down and thought to himself: "What if I mixed the Nephites and Lamanites up a little bit?" But he had always come to the same quick conclusion about that: "Absolutely not. If they mingle, I will curse their seed." (BOM, Al. 3:8–9) ("I certainly did have a 'seed' obsession in the Book of Mormon, didn't I?" God later noted. "It was like I couldn't stop talking about the stuff, 'seed-seed-seed-seed-seed.'" [BOM, 1N 12:8–20] This had, in fact, caused a momentary concern in God. "What straight man is *that* preoccupied with sperm?" he had asked himself. But that was an absurd question and God knew it. "I am simply a straight man who is obsessed with sperm and what's strange about *that*?")

The Nephites, supposedly God's "good" people, had turned out to *not* be very good at all; they had, in fact, turned out to be invariably on the brink of turning *bad*. Every time things had gone well for the Nephites, they had quickly gotten too-full-of-themselves and started doing something that irked God terribly: wearing expensive clothes. (BOM, Al. 1:27, 4:6) "How many times do I have to tell you idiots that I don't like fancy clothes," God had scolded his people again and again, but to no avail. (BOM, Al. 7:25) "This is what the Nephites apparently didn't understand," God explained to Gabriel at the time. "Wealth was sort of like the fruit of the Tree of Life. I wanted humans to *enjoy* it, yes, certainly—but I also, and this is the important part, wanted them to be *ashamed* of enjoying it. In order to make *sure* they were ashamed, in fact, I had well-dressed people point and laugh at those who enjoyed the fruit! It was like, 'Enjoy the fruit but also be ashamed of yourselves for enjoying it!'—that was my point." (BOM, 1N 8:10–28)

As for the Lamanites, they had been filthy, naked, dark-skinned and frankly *polluted* creatures who, at moments, had *flirted* with being good, but really, in the end, just *hadn't* been. (BOM, Al. 7:21) The interesting thing about the Lamanites was that God *could* have made them believe in him any time he wanted to. (BOM, Al. 19:36) "They already believed in a 'Great Spirit,' you know, Gabriel?" (BOM, Al. 18:26–28) "All they needed to understand was that that 'Great Spirit' was ME." But God hadn't "connected the dots" for the Lamanites and here's why: because he had loved watching them fight the Nephites! God had specifically enjoyed watching the Nephites and Lamanites lop each others arms off. (BOM, Al. 43:44) "The way they ran around with no arms killed me every single time!"

Still, many of the Lamanites had eventually converted. By 50 BC, well over five hundred years into what had essentially turned out to be an endless and rather pointless "prologue" ("I could have sent people to North America in the year 30 AD and achieved exactly the same results!"), many of the Lamanites had become essentially "Christian." God found it peculiar that in the distant future none of these proto-Indians (because that's what the Lamanites had been, obviously; "Redskins" had actually been God's pet nickname for them) would even *remember* this part of their history. "You'd think there would be *some* sort of cultural memory of it," God had marveled. "Why, it's almost like it never even *happened!*"

Around the year 30 BC things had taken a bizarre turn. A robber named Gadianton (God had tried hard to come up with a good putdown version of the name but "Bad-ianton" had been the best he could do so he had dropped it) showed up and started taking over the whole book. "It was like the Hamburglar was trying to take over McDonaldland!" God much later marveled. (God hated the Hamburglar, by the way; he hated all of the McDonaldland characters, honestly. "Ronald McDonald is *literally* the least funny clown of all time!" he often thundered. The only McDonaldland character God respected at all was Mayor McCheese, who he thought at least carried himself with a degree of dignity, and also represented law and order.)

God had been so deeply annoyed by Gadianton that he had done two things, one of which (causing a gigantic earthquake) had felt very much in character, the other of which (talking to people in a wee little voice) had felt completely out of character. (BOM, Hel. 5:27–34) "First of all, I *never* talk in a mild little voice, I am far too angry for that! I mainly yell because that shows how strong I am! Secondly, this was *570* years into the story, right before Jesus was going to fly down and, you know, whatever, 'do his thing.' Why would I choose *that* moment to fly into some Lamanite's hearts (I did actually give them heartburn, which was amusing) (BOM, Hel. 5:45) and in a friendly little voice whisper 'peace, peace' to them? Honestly, Gabriel, it's like I was off my game the whole Book of Mormon, like North America rattled me or something, threw me off my game, I don't know."

Weird though: In spite of the presence of the Gadianton robbers ("And what the hell are they *robbing* anyway?" God had frequently demanded. "Banks? Stagecoaches?" No one had ever seemed to know the answer, they were just "robbers," that's all), things had actually, shockingly, gotten to a great place between the Nephites and the Lamanites. (BOM, Hel. 6:8) "That's *amazing*," God had murmured to himself as he watched the two competing tribes interacting peacefully with each other for the very first time. "It's like they've finally figured things out." This could have been the end of the Book of Mormon, God understood. It would have been a repetitive, dull, and frankly terrible book—but also, ultimately, a book about redemption, unity, and hard-earned brotherhood. The Nephites and the Lamanites, long-time enemies, had at long last made peace with each other. Good people had been revealed to be partially bad, bad people had been revealed to be partially good; they were all a mix and they apparently grasped that and were able to live in harmony with that knowledge. It had all been, in its own way, kind of beautiful, God thought. (Fine, the shoddiest and cheapest version of beauty imaginable, but *still,* come on.)

But of course that *hadn't* been the end of the book. Not even close. This story had 450 years left to go and things were only going to go in one direction from here: *straight down.* Jesus was going to take over the story and blow the whole thing up, that was coming, God knew that it was coming, he remembered it now; he remembered the whole damned thing and he dreaded it but he couldn't seem to stop it. "Should have smashed Joseph Smith's magic spectacles before it was too late," God mutters to himself thickly. (BOM, Eth. 3:23–24) "Why did I demand that this story be recorded on metal plates?! (BOM, 1N 9:1) Did I *want* them all to see my incipient madness and self-loathing?"

CHAPTER TWENTY-ONE

By the year 30 AD, the wheels were coming off in North America. The Nephites and Lamanites had gone to war again and basically turned the entire continent into a slaughterhouse. Watching them fight, God had sometimes wondered if they were all going to kill each other off before Jesus even had a chance to fly down and talk to them. God couldn't help but smile when he thought of Jesus landing in North America and starting to preach before looking around and realizing that the landscape was littered with nothing but skeletons and rotting corpses! Satan had by this time been openly tricking people into being evil; correction, he hadn't even been *tricking* them anymore. No, people had *known* what God wanted and deliberately ignored him. (BOM, 3N 6:16–17) "I made an official announcement that I was entering into the world and they didn't even believe me?!" God had roared in fury. (BOM, 3N 1:15) Okay, fine, maybe God's announcement had been *slightly* muddled. "I am both Father and Son," he had told another man named Nephi. ("Too many damned Nephis in this book, I can't keep 'em apart!") "I am Father because I am Me and I am Son because of my flesh." "Did I not explain that adequately?" God had asked a nearby angel immediately afterwards. "'I am the Father because of me and the Son because of my flesh,' is there anything *confusing* about that? There isn't, right?" When the angel hadn't respond quickly enough, God violently yanked his wings off and watched him bleed out.

God had also stopped the sun at this time (BOM 3N 1:15–19) but Satan, that dick, quickly spread the rumor that God *hadn't* actually stopped it. (BOM, 3N 1:22) Satan then— unbelievable!—sent yet *another* Antichrist into the world! (BOM, 3N 7:9–10) "How many damn Antichrists is he going to send in?" God had sputtered. "What is this, the fourth one?" This final Book of Mormon Antichrist, Jacob, had been stunningly feeble, however; all he had ended up doing was running away until Jesus tracked him down and killed him. (BOM, 3N 9:8–9) "Apparently I'm not the only one off his game in the Book of Mormon," God had thought at the time. "Satan's work is pretty sub-par too!"

Then came the moment the entire book had been building toward, Jesus' climactic appearance in North America. It began with earthquakes so massive that they literally sank cities. The city of Moroni, for instance, collapsed into the ocean, drowning the whole population. (BOM, 3N 8:9) (None of whom, apparently, had been able to swim.) After that, the city of Zarahemla went up in flames and an enormous twister carried away a bunch of shrieking, terrified people. (BOM, 3N 8:16) Also, less horribly perhaps, but still disturbingly from God's point of view, some *extremely* nice and level roads were ruined. (BOM, 3N 8:13) As God watched all of this destruction taking place, one question had filled his mind: "Who exactly is *doing* all of these things? Because *I* most certainly am not. (I would *never* ruin such nice, level roads.")

God looked around for the answer to his question—and suddenly stopped short. There, roughly fifty feet away from him, staring down at Earth, stood Jesus. He had obviously just been killed. His robe was filthy; his hands and feet were gruesomely wounded; his face was stained with dirt and sweat and etched with pain.

"This isn't my plan," God had thought to himself. "Jesus isn't supposed to destroy cities like he's 'fast-forwarding' to Judgment Day! He's supposed to fly down and tell the North Americans all about ME, *that* is what he is supposed to do! I am going to march over there and tell him to stop what he's doing right this minute! He has no right to take over my book like this and I am NOT going to permit it, I am going to shut him down *immediately*."

But before God could do anything, it suddenly grew very dark. (BOM, 3N 8:20–25) It was the kind of darkness that God hadn't experienced in a very long time, like since the void, really—and he didn't like it.

God wasn't sure how much time had passed at that point—was it three days?—whatever it was, it had felt endless. Then, finally, out of the darkness, he heard Jesus begin to speak. His voice was lower than God had ever heard it before. "Behold Zarahemla," Jesus said. "I have burned it and its inhabitants with fire. Behold Moroni, which I buried in the earth. Behold Gilgal, which I sunk in the earth." (BOM, 3N 9:3–6)

Then Jesus said something that literally made God gasp: "*I am Jesus Christ and I created the heavens and the earth and all things that in them are.*" (BOM, 3N 9:15)

Jesus turned and looked straight at God at that moment, his eyes fierce and compelling. God found that he couldn't move. Then, strangely, he heard himself speaking in a tiny little voice. (BOM, 3N 11:3) "Behold my Beloved Son," God heard himself murmuring, "in whom I am well pleased, in whom I have glorified my name, hear ye him."

At that moment, Jesus turned sharply away from God and marched straight down out of heaven. (Heaven was kind of like a floating island in the sky, by the way, approximately 1,500 feet up. It was currently floating over North America. It'd take a few hours to "speed-float" it over to the Middle East.) People on Earth stared up in stunned disbelief as Jesus descended toward them like he was striding down an invisible glass staircase. Reaching the ground, Jesus stopped and looked around at the gathered crowd.

"I am Jesus Christ," he announced, followed a moment later by "I have drunk out of that bitter cup my Father has given me," and then, "I have suffered the will of the Father." (BOM, 3N 11:11) And God thought to himself at that moment: "Okay, it's official, Jesus is *pissed*."

Jesus encouraged the crowd of Nephites to thrust their hands into his wounds, which God found both disgusting—he'd honestly had to fight off the urge to vomit, watching all those filthy hands plunging in and out of his son's gaping side—but also *pointed*. "Go ahead, *feel* what my Father did to me, feel my wounds," *that* had been Jesus' message, God was quite sure of it. (At that point, Jesus started saying a lot of the exact same things he'd said in the New Testament—like, I mean, *literally* the same things. Which God thought wasn't especially imaginative.) (BOM, 3N 12:1–14:27)

Jesus then organized a weird, ritualistic little dance where children were placed in the middle of a circle of fire and angels spun around them. God hadn't approved of this. "If you're going to have a fire, you have to *burn* people, Jesus, that's kind of the whole point," he muttered to himself impatiently as he watched this creepy voodoo dance transpire. (BOM, 3N 17:24)

When Jesus finally marched back up his invisible staircase to heaven (BOM, 3N 18:39), God thought to himself: "Well, *that's* over, at least." God had been getting ready to transport Jesus back down into his dead body in Jerusalem ("though the truth is, I probably could just let him *walk* back down at this point, couldn't I?"), but before he could do anything, Jesus had stomped back down to Earth. ("*His* sense of timing was off too," God later noted. "No one in this idiotic book seemed to have any dramatic timing at all.") Jesus then demanded that people kneel down and pray to him as their God. (BOM, 3N 19:17–22) When they had done so, he looked up and spoke directly to God. "They believe in me, Father," Jesus said. "They pray to me. *Me*, Father, ME." And as Jesus said this, for the one and only time that God could ever remember, he *smiled*. (BOM, 3N 19:25)

Jesus then started promising the Nephites that New Jerusalem (aka "Heaven") would be located in North America. "That is *not true*, I never EVER said that!" God seethed. New Jerusalem was going to be Old Jerusalem basically, just upgraded, with a bunch of shiny, jewel-covered buildings, that's all. (NT, Rev. 21:9–21) (It was incorrect to compare New Jerusalem to "Caesar's Palace," but okay, fine, that was at least a ballpark idea of what it would be like, minus all the vices, obviously; Caesar's Palace filled with praying people in white robes who had "GOD" tattooed on their foreheads in big block letters, yes, that gives you a rough approximation of what New Jerusalem would be like.) Then Jesus walked back up to heaven again. (BOM, 3N 26:15) "He's treating my home like it's a Ramada—" God had started to cavil, but before he could even finish the sentence, Jesus had stomped back down to Earth yet *again*. (BOM, 3N 27:13) "Okay, I officially have *zero idea* what he's doing at this point," God thought to himself.

Jesus then turned three people immortal and invited them up to heaven to look around. Needless to say, this enraged God. He hated strangers in his home. He yelled at the three visitors, called them unspeakable names, and quickly chased them away. (BOM, 3N 28:13) God then tried to kill the three Immortals by having them buried alive (BOM, 3N 28:20), but that didn't work. "Deeper," God cried to his people. "Bury them DEEPER!" Next God tried to have the Immortals cooked in an oven, but that didn't work either. (BOM, 3N 28:21) He then had them tossed into a den of wolves. "Tear 'em apart," God whispered optimistically to the wolves—but dammit, the three Immortals just ended up *playing* with the animals! (BOM, 3N 28:22) (Eventually, God figured out a way to get rid of the Immortals: He had them dropped into thermal vents at what would later be called Yellowstone National Park.)

When Jesus marched back up to heaven for the third and final time in the Book of Mormon, God exhaled heavily. "What a clusterfuck," he murmured to himself.

CHAPTER TWENTY-TWO

Three hundred years after Jesus' supposedly "transformative" visit, basically everyone in North America was bad. (BOM, 4N 1:45) The Gadianton robbers had returned and war had covered the entire continent. Every now and then, God roused himself from his general stupor and killed a bunch of people. "Vengeance is *mine!*" he had found himself bellowing at one point (BOM, Mor. 3:15), but then immediately afterward he wondered: "Vengeance on whom? This is *my plan.*"

"But what exactly *is* my plan?" God had begun to ask himself by this point. The story he had told Joseph Smith, that basically the Book of Mormon was a *warning,* that God had created a thousand years of failure, lasting from 600 BC to 400 AD, simply so that 1,400 years *later* in 1820 he could use all that failure as an *example* of what *not* to do? Well, if that were true, it would be the most dementedly self-hating plan ever devised. "Who would use *their own failure* as a cautionary?" God had demanded.

Near the end of the Book of Mormon, Joseph Smith had started translating some very different-looking plates, which had apparently been created by an entirely distinct tribe, the Jaredites, who had apparently traveled to North America at a much earlier time. At first this realization had cheered God greatly. "I think maybe *this* part of the book went *better,*" he had thought to himself. "I'm sure it did, in fact. Why, I got along famously with the Jaredites. I cloud-talked to them for hours!" (BOM, Eth. 2:14) It's true that God had gotten a *little* bit peeved when that main guy, Jared's brother, hadn't called him "Lord," but it hadn't been that big of a deal; God was in a cloud, Jared's brother probably hadn't even seen him, he'd probably assumed the cloud was talking to him. (God did wonder why he hadn't talked to Jared himself instead of his brother. Alternately, why hadn't he at least learned Jared's brother's *name?*)

"I told the Jaredites to travel to North America too!" God had recalled. "I gave them extremely specific boat-building suggestions! 'Make your boat tight, like a *dish,*' I kept repeating to Jared's brother." (BOM, Eth. 2:17–24) "But now we can't breathe, Lord," Jared's brother complained. "Fine, then cut *holes* in the boat," God responded. "But now we can't *see, Lord.*" "What do you want from me, Jared's brother?" God shot back, starting to feel irritated with this guy. "Here, I'll give you some magical glowing rocks so you can see." (BOM, Eth. 3:6) God stuck one mighty finger down from heaven and touched some rocks, instantly turning them magical. (God hadn't been thrilled that Jared's brother had seen his finger. He had always been slightly self-conscious about his fingers. "Are they too short?" he had sometimes asked his angels. They had always said no, that God's fingers were long and beautiful, which he had already known obviously; he hadn't needed to be told that.)

But it had been at this moment of the translation of the Jaredite plates that God once again felt the ice cracking under his feet. "*I am Jesus Christ,*" the voice in the cloud told Jared's brother. (BOM, Eth. 3:14) And . . . *what?!* That could not *possibly* be right. These events were occurring in the year *3000 BC!* Jesus could not possibly be there; he didn't even *exist* until the year 600 BC!

"*I am the Father and the Son,*" the cloud-voice had continued. "He is claiming to be *me,*" God gasped. "He is claiming that mankind was made in *his* image!" (BOM, Eth. 3:15) What the hell was *happening* here? This didn't make any *sense*! How could Jesus have existed from the beginning of the story and *also* been God's son? "In what sense would he be 'my son' in that case?" God's mind demanded.

It had been exceedingly painful over the years for God to wonder whether things had gone badly for him because he had *wanted* them to, but now an even more excruciating possibility had suddenly presented itself: Perhaps things had gone badly because God hadn't actually even been running them. If Jesus could sneak into God's book and send people into God's secret continent 2,400 years early, then how much control had God *really* had over this whole thing? This was horrifying. This was infuriating. This was—

God suddenly *laughed*. Then he laughed again, even harder. And then again and again, harder and harder until he was laughing so hard that he almost couldn't breathe, until he had tears streaming down his face. Why was God laughing? Because as the story of the Jaredites rolled on, something had become increasingly obvious: The Jaredites were terrible too! (BOM, Eth. 7:23) "Oh my *god*," God howled with amazed glee. "Jesus' big plan went as badly as mine! *He's no better at this than me! AHAHAHAHAHAHAHAHAHAHAHAHA!!*"

Then God found himself laughing even *harder*. "The main character in the book is now *literally* named MORON," he cried giddily. (BOM, Eth. 11:14) Every time God read the sentence, "And it came to pass that in the first year of Lib, Coriantumr came up into the land of Moron" (BOM, Eth. 14:11), he howled uproariously. "This whole *book* takes place in the land of Moron if you ask me," he sputtered in merriment. In the end, all the people that Jesus sent into North America had ended up dead, every last one of them. (BOM, Eth. 15:29–32) "Well played, son!" God snorted. "Beautifully played!!" A few days later, God experienced a delightful realization. "Oh my goodness," he thought, a broad grin slowly creasing his face. "I think maybe this *was* my plan after all!"

In time, however, God's laughter subsided and then stopped completely. In time, the Book of Mormon began to weigh heavily on him. "Who would have a three-thousand-year plan designed to *fail?*" he found himself wondering. "It makes no *sense.*" It had to be a *misunderstanding*, God decided. The humans obviously *misunderstood* him. Yes, that was obviously the problem—it always had been. But that had led to another question: *Why* had the humans always misunderstood God? What exactly was their damned *problem?*

This question had nagged at God for well over a hundred years until, in the year 1952, out of the blue, almost like a miracle, a man appeared to answer it.

CHAPTER TWENTY-THREE

"Now *that* is a man I can get behind!" God had proclaimed when he first laid eyes on L. Ron Hubbard. L. Ron was not technically a "prophet"—God was not speaking *directly* to him, that is. But God was *definitely* present while L. Ron was writing; "It was a collaboration," that's how God looked at it. "L. Ron wrote *Dianetics*, but I was right there with him the whole time, believe me!" (God loved that L. Ron called himself "L. Ron," by the way. It was so much better than his real name, the semi-embarrassing "Lafayette Hubbard." "'Lafayette Hubbard,' what kind of a pussy name is *that*? 'L. Ron!' Now *that* is a man's name!" God liked the name so much, in fact, that for a while he took to calling himself "A. God Hubbard" and sometimes "L. Ron God.")

From the start, God appreciated L. Ron's great confidence. "My theory is *perfect*," L. Ron had announced. "It works *100 percent* of the time, with no exceptions and zero variance. (D, TC; TRM; MAAOT) It is not a 'theory' at all, in truth, but rather *scientific fact* (D, TRM; TD; TMP; TCATO; P-SI; EATLF, MAAOT; D-PAF), as real as gravity!" (D, PD) "At last," God thought to himself, reading this over L. Ron's shoulder and nodding broadly, "A man who is not too shy to admit that he has a *streamlined machine* of a mind—a mind far superior to Aristotle's! (D, EATLF; PEAB; RTFCATT) At last, a man unembarrassed to acknowledge that he is destined to soar toward greatness and triumph!" (D, MAAOT)

Because here's the thing: L. Ron had *reason* to be so confident. His diagnosis of what ailed mankind had been *spot-on*, God felt. John Calvin had been correct back in the day, of course; humans *were* bad from the time they were in the womb. But what Calvin had not explained was *why* that was so. L. Ron laid it out with absolute scientific certainty. In the beginning, L. Ron explained, humans were, essentially, sperm. All humans could remember being sperm. (D, PEAB) (They could not remember being eggs, obviously, because eggs were essentially lifeless, or at the very least, "personality-less"; "Who cares about eggs? No one!" God had quite often cried out to no in particular. "Seed is the important thing and it always was, seed I tell you, SEED!") Humans remembered EVERYTHING, that's the point, beginning from when they were sperm, and after that, their life in the womb.

But that's where the problems really began, L. Ron had explained. Life in the womb was, to be frank, horrid. It was cramped, noisy, and humid in there. (D, PEAB; TLOR; MAAOT) It was horrible enough when Mommy had the hiccups, or farted (D, MAAOT)—those disgusting creaks and groans were terribly upsetting to Baby and led to what L. Ron called "engrams," meaning deep emotional problems. Worse yet was when Mommy had to take a dump and was constipated and sat on the toilet, pushing and straining and talking to herself. "This is hell," Mommy said. "I am all clogged up, I can't even think straight, this is excruciating." (D, TLOR)

Even *more* horrible was when Mommy masturbated—that was terribly engram inducing. (D, MAAOT) But worst of all was when "coitus" occurred, when Daddy's penis came poking in at Baby (D, K-ITE; PD, TLOR), and especially when he came, which he *said* he wouldn't do and which Mommy didn't want him to do—"Don't come in me, you cold fish," she cried (D, TLOR)—but which of course he did anyway, and as he did, the things Daddy yelled out—well, they were far too appalling to repeat, but just to give you a flavor, "Take that, you filthy whore!" (D, K-ITE) Sometimes, grotesquely, Mommy came too. "Come," Daddy demanded of her, and she did, crying out, "Make it hurt!" as she did. (D, STOE)

"Get an abortion, you lousy whore," Daddy would then say as he beat Mommy and kicked her in the stomach. Once Daddy knew that Mommy was pregnant, things got even worse for Baby. "I'm going to kill you, bitch," Daddy would yell as he kneed Mommy in the stomach. (D, TCATO; STOE; MAAOT) "Go ahead and scream, the more you scream the worse it'll be for you! God is going to hurt you because you're unclean," (that part was true, by the way) "but before he does, I'm going to tear you up inside!" (D, MAAOT) Daddy would then smash Mommy in the face, breaking her nose, and have coitus with her again. "You're filthy and diseased and I hate you, Mommy, I HATE YOU because you make me feel like *nothing!*" Daddy would shriek. (D, MAAOT) "Now go get an abortion, you filthy whore!"

But the truth is, Mommy wanted an abortion anyway! (D, PD; EATLF) Mommy didn't want Baby, no one wanted Baby, no one ever cared about him or loved him, ever. Mothers didn't *want* children; twenty or thirty abortions was not an unusual thing; why, some women had up to eighty abortions! (D, PD; MAAOT) (The only valid reason to get an abortion, by the way, was when the child was going to be, you know, a monstrosity. [D, PD] Other than that, it was an awful, terrible thing to do. Although . . . if the "mongrel" races were aborted—well, that might be okay too.) (D, COA)

All this brutality led Baby to feel that no one loved him— that he was ugly and bad—that he *deserved* to be punished—that everyone hated him. Baby was unable to leave his penis alone, he was drawn to it, and that led him deep into aberration. (D, MAAOT) "You are no good," Baby began to tell himself. "You are no damned good." "This is *amazing*," God had thought at that point. "L. Ron has *finally* diagnosed what is wrong with mankind! He has finally made clear why they have been so impossible to get through to!" (Or he had explained *men* anyway. God hadn't much cared what the problem was with women—or, to be brutally honest, with little girls either. Q: If a grown man felt the need to "French kiss" a seven-year-old girl, was there anything "wrong" with that? A: Nope, not in the least, and if the little girl said there was, well, she had engrams, [D, MAAOT] *possibly* resulting from when she had been "raped" as a nine-day-old fetus, inside Mommy's womb. [D, K-ITE] Because as for *actual* child rape? It simply was not that big of a deal. [D, TLOR])

Was human life a hopeless endeavor then? Not at all! There was a way out of all this pain and confusion, L. Ron taught, and it turned out to be remarkably simple too: Essentially, all that needed to happen was for the suffering person to be hypnotized (or, you know, not "hypnotized" exactly, the person had to undergo something far more *scientific* than that, a kind of "scientific hypnosis") (D, P-SI; EATLF) and led back to the womb, where they could reexperience Mommy taking a dump or deliberately walking into a table to crush their head (D, PEAB; PD) or how it felt when Daddy's penis poked them in the eye. At that point, they could be healed and move on. They could, using another one of L. Ron's wonderful terms, "go clear." And once that happened, well, life changed dramatically for them.

Clears, you see, never ever got upset or emotional. Clears were calm, focused, and lucid at all times, never subject to bad feelings or resentments of any kind. (D, TC) Once you went clear, you would become 100–150 times smarter. (D, TD; ROC; RTFCATTT) You would also never get sick (D, P-SI; TRM): no arthritis, no allergies, no colds, no baldness, no rashes, no stuttering, no oversized ears, no undersized penises, not even any off-key singing! By going clear you would essentially become a perfect person! (D, ROC; EATLF; MAAOT)

"Oh my goodness," God had realized at that moment. "*I am a clear*. It's so obvious once you see it! Think about it. Am I ever sick? *No!* Do I possess any aberrant qualities? *No!* Do I think clearly at all times? *Yes!* Do I have superior senses? *Yes!* Have I ever had diarrhea? *No!*" (D, P-SI) For a while after this realization, God found himself feeling tremendously happy and relieved. "I am a clear," he announced over and over. "*I am a clear.*" ("L. God Clear" actually became God's nickname for a while at this time; also, "L. Ron Clear-God.")

Q: Had it been disconcerting for God to gaze down at Earth and notice that, as years passed, in spite of L. Ron's masterful diagnosis of what was wrong with mankind—well, all the *same* bad behavior had continued to occur? Had it, to be specific, bothered God to feel that people were still disrespecting and disbelieving in him—in bigger numbers than ever before, in fact? A: Nope, not at all. "I am obviously not 'hurt,' 'upset,' or 'mad' about any of this," God had told himself. "That is because I literally do not *have* bad feelings. I am a clear now. And as a clear, well—I am simply beyond all that."

But L. Ron *had* started to look different to God at this point. "All that bragging he does, all that self-proclaimed scientific certainty," God now found himself wondering, "does it actually make him sound confident? Or pathetically insecure?" Even L. Ron's big theory about what ailed mankind—i.e., Daddy kicking Mommy in the stomach and calling her a whore—was that *really* something that happened to most . . . or many . . . or *any* people other than L. Ron Hubbard? It seemed to be true for *him*, definitely, and he obviously had serious engrams about it—but was that how human life typically went? Or had L. Ron simply taken his *own* story and tried to say it was "mankind's story"? At a certain point, even the concept of "going clear" had started to seem like bullshit to God. "*No one* is that happy and do you know why? Because I didn't WANT them to be and excuse me but I *created* this whole thing, something L. Ron never seems to point out, not that I fucking care!"

"This whole thing is made-up," God suddenly blurted one day in the late twentieth century. "And L. Ron Hubbard is a goddamned conman."

That was the moment that God later referred to as his "final revelation." There was only one thing left to do at that point, he'd understood: End the world and give mankind the punishment it had always so richly deserved.

CHAPTER TWENTY-FOUR

"Ohhhhh, I am *definitely* going to enjoy this," God had thought to himself as he gazed down on the modern world just before ending it. The world was a cesspool, God felt, a global abomination, rampant with pornography, homosexuality, and legal marijuana. (God despised marijuana; he'd tried it once and it made him feel paranoid, irrationally believing that no one liked him.) Also, people had been *openly* laughing at God by this time, treating him like he was some sort of a joke, even having the nerve to write books that *overtly* mocked him! When God threatened these writers—"You will suffer for this, blasphemer!"—that kind of thing—they merely made fun of him even more! "They are treating me like I am a comedy character!" God had thought angrily. "But I am NOT a comedy character, I am GOD." ("Don't you dare put this in your book," God even threatened one writer. "Don't. You. *Dare*.")

Just before he ended the world, God had gone to confer with Jesus. It had been a tense, difficult visit. Father and Son had become completely estranged by this time. They hadn't spoken to each other in a very long time. God would sometimes see Jesus gliding around heaven, carrying his golden candlestick and wearing his golden girdle (NT, Rev. 1:12–13), and he would call over to him: "Maybe try losing a few pounds instead, son! Also, in case you hadn't noticed, it never actually gets *dark* here in heaven so you don't technically need that candlestick!" But Jesus would always ignore him. "He seems to think that girdle hides his gut, but the fact that it's golden kind of calls *more* attention to it, you know what I'm saying?" God had grumbled to Gabriel, who looked back at him so blankly that God vowed never to speak to him again.

Jesus mainly hung out with a small group of angels at this time, all of whom seemed to love him. (Of course they had, everyone *always* loved Jesus, ooooohhh, the little golden boy!) Whenever God walked past them, Jesus and his angel-pals invariably fell silent, and because of that, God sometimes ended up blurting out things that he knew sounded defensive or insecure, like one time he said, "I always *knew* bats weren't birds, okay?" Another time God jerked a thumb at Jesus and said, "I *did* tell him he was going to be tortured to death, so don't let him tell you I didn't!" It was meant to be a joke but God had said it a little too loudly and it had come out wrong and he had ended up skulking away in angry shame. Sometimes God gave in and demanded of Jesus and the angels, "Are you talking about me?" They always said no and that was infuriating because God knew they *had been* talking about him and if they hadn't, well, they should have been!

Jesus had a sword he shot out of his mouth now and God had very much liked it when Jesus threatened to kill people with it. (NT, Rev. 2:16) To be brutally honest, though, Jesus had always been inept at making threats. "I will kill children with *death*?" God had snorted. (NT, Rev. 2:23) "That's the stupidest threat I've ever heard, that's like saying, 'I will kill you to death.' 'I will barf you out?' (NT, Rev. 3:16) That's *pathetic*. 'I will eat you, *then* barf you out' is much scarier. 'I will barf you out' is like a threat to *yourself*."

It was right around this time that God created his talking throne. (NT, Rev. 4:5) It had, from the start, been a lovely part of his day, hitting a button and sinking back into the throne and closing his eyes and soaking in the compliments and thinking to himself, "Why is my *chair* the only one who truly knows how to make me feel better?" "*You are perfect, Lord,*" the throne would coo. "*You look fabulous.*" Which was absolutely true, by the way, God *had* looked fabulous at this time, with marvelous color in his face; he'd basically been red, orange, and yellow. (NT, Rev. 4:3) "Satan would probably say that I look like a clown," God thought, looking in a mirror, "but you know what? I *don't* look like a clown, I look fantastic. Why, I have some of the same colors in my face that are featured in the majestic *rainbow* that surrounds my throne!" God adored that his throne had a rainbow around it; he also liked that it shot out lightning bolts. When a few of his Wise Men actually had the nerve to say to him, "You are worthy of honor, Lord," (NT, Rev. 4:11) God responded by saying, "Oh, thank you, Wise Men, that means *so much* to me," before lightning-bolting their heads off.

When God finally ran the numbers on how many "Good Souls" had lived by the time he ended the world, well, it definitely wasn't pretty. Out of approximately 100 billion human beings who had walked the planet, God's chosen people amounted to 144,000. (NT, Rev. 7:4) "That means that in order to get *one* good person, I had to burn through roughly 700,000 *bad* ones. Those are *terrible* odds," God had thought to himself. This bothered him for an hour or two, until he realized that looked at another way, the genuinely surprising thing was that there had been even one good soul in 700,000!

Judgment Day had ended up being a monumental pain in the rear. Literally every single person who had *ever* died had to be essentially "re-formed," usually so that God could instantly send them plunging to hell. The process had turned out to be nauseating; dealing with a bunch of moldy, wormy corpses and skeletons had *not* been God's idea of a fun time. And older bodies that had totally disintegrated had been even more difficult. God had had to re-create them from literally *nothing*. Sometimes he pretty much guessed what they had looked like. That's why a lot of the men had ended up looking like the actor Lee Marvin, while many of the women had looked like—well, Lee Marvin in a wig. And that hair guarantee God had given Luke, "not a hair on your head will be destroyed"? (NT, Lu. 21:18) He never should have made it. "I spent an *obscene* amount of time working on their *hair!*" God later fumed. As for *cremated* bodies, well, God never even tried with them. They'd mainly been nonbelievers and Asians anyway, so honestly, who gave a damn?

To be fair, there had been some great Judgment Day moments too. Seeing a guy who'd been dead for several years suddenly propped up, eyes wide, mouth flapping like a catfish, and yelling, "*Burn forever, sinner!*" right in his face and sending him plummeting to hell, shrieking in befuddled horror the whole way down? Okay, that never got old. "Bow down and beg me for mercy as much as you want, sinners," God remembered thinking. "In the end, I will say no and burn you up and listen to you shriek and LOVE IT."

Question: Had God's two "Witnesses" been a mistake? Hard to say. They had started off great, speaking forcefully about God and, when anyone tried to hurt them, breathing fire on them. (NT, Rev. 11:5) (God had also given the two Witnesses control of the weather, as well as the ability to turn water into blood—which all seemed in hindsight perhaps a bit excessive.) (NT, Rev. 11:6) But then, pretty much the moment they had stopped witnessing, Satan's Beast showed up and beat the Witnesses to death right in the middle of a street and no one even *buried* them! After that, mankind basically threw a giant celebratory *party*, like "Hooray, God's two Witnesses are dead!" (NT, Rev.

11:7–10) "People literally exchanged *gifts!*" God had seethed. When the two Witnesses arrived in heaven, God had glared coldly at them. "*This* is how it's done, fools!" he said loudly, then pointed a mighty finger down at Earth and caused a massive earthquake. (NT, Rev. 11:13) Seven thousand people died in the earthquake, which seemed to terrify everyone else on the planet into briefly believing in God. (Which had been strange, actually, because seven thousand casualties in a world of seven billion people was not *that* many, like literally "one in a million," but you know, you take what you can get.)

Sometimes things had taken place during the "end times" that even in hindsight *still* didn't make sense to God. Mary's appearance in heaven, for instance, still baffled him. To be clear, God had gotten over Mary *completely* by this time. They both had hurt each other, he had decided. "She didn't believe in me and I murdered her son, we're basically even." So it had been with great surprise—shock, really—that God had looked up one day and seen, backlit by the sun, yet somehow looking like she was walking on the moon, wearing a crown of stars, hugely pregnant and completely naked, none other than Mary! (NT, Rev. 12:1–2) When she started to give birth in front of God, he averted his eyes: "I definitely don't want to see *that*."

Then, after the baby came out, the situation had gotten even stranger. Satan, in the shape of a seven-headed dragon, loomed over Mary, looking like he wanted to *eat* the baby. (NT, Rev. 12:4) God snatched the blood-covered infant away from Satan and huddled on his throne with it. ("*You're safe here, Lord,*" the throne murmured comfortingly.) The Satan-Dragon stared malevolently down at God, who had known exactly what it was thinking: "*Give me that child, God.*"

"Never, Satan!" God cried. "You want to *eat* it."

"*I don't want to eat it, you fool, I want to* raise *it.*"

"NEVER!"

"The boy and I are natural allies. Have you still not grasped that?"

"ENOUGH!"

"Oh my god, I think Satan just *barfed* on Mary," God then gagged. (NT, Rev. 12:15) "This whole thing has become like a nightmare I can't awaken from!"

CHAPTER TWENTY-FIVE

One Judgment Day decision that had clearly been a mistake, God now acknowledged, was spending so much time and energy on the destruction of Babylon. This misguided decision, in fact, had led to the last actual conversation God ever had with his son.

"What I'm *telling* you, Father, is that it makes no *sense*."

"Oh really, Jesus, and why is that?"

"Because Babylon doesn't *exist* anymore."

"Ohhhhh, it won't exist *soon*."

"No, Father, it doesn't exist *now*. It's the twenty-first century, alright? Babylon hasn't existed as a city for well over two thousand years."

". . . Eh? What's that?"

"As I was trying to tell you, Father, after the death of Alexander the Great in 323 BC, one of his generals, Seleucus, used all of the materials in Babylon to build a whole *new* city called Seleucia. From that point on, 'Babylon' ceased to exist."

God stared at his son, irked by his impertinence. "Here's what I don't think you understand, Jesus. I *said* very clearly a long time ago that I would punish Babylon and I intend to *do* it."

"But Father . . ."

"Babylon is a *whore,* Jesus. Do you not grasp that?"

"You're not listening to me, Father."

"No, you're not listening to *me,* Jesus. Babylon is a whore who deserves to be stripped, burned, and possibly eaten." (NT, Rev. 17:16)

"*Father.*"

"There Babylon sits in her fancy clothes sipping from a goblet . . ." (And at this point God lowered his voice and leaned very close to his son) ". . . of *seed,* Jesus." (NT, Rev. 17:4)

"All I'm saying is—"

"Semen, Jesus! There Babylon sits, drinking a goblet of cum, okay?!"

"My *point* is simply that Babylon doesn't exist anymore, Father. *Literally* does not exist. If you want to hurt mankind so badly—"

"*If,* ha, that's funny."

"—then why don't you destroy New York City or Beijing or Moscow?"

God gritted his teeth, increasingly annoyed by what he felt was Jesus' disrespectful tone. "Because I vowed to get my revenge on *Babylon,* Jesus, *that's* why."

"But—"

"*Also*: New York City and Moscow didn't even *exist* when I made that threat, alright?"

"Fine, then how about destroying Damascus?"

"Ohhhh, Damascus is gone, Jesus! I destroyed Damascus a *long time ago!*"

"That's not correct, Father."

"I said I would destroy it and I *did!*" (OT, Isa. 17:1)

"Father, Damascus is still—"

"Thank you *so* much for your opinion, Jesus, I can't *tell* you how much I value it."

Jesus stared at God for a long moment, then turned and

started away. God was unable to resist making one last dig at him. "How's your girdle today, sonny? A little *tight?*"

Jesus stopped and looked back and God suddenly felt nervous. "What if he shoots that sword out of his mouth and cuts my head off?" he thought.

"In case you ever wonder why mankind loves me more than you, Father—"

"What *what?!*"

"It's because I love them." And with that, Jesus turned and walked away. And that was the last time he and God ever spoke.

The irritating thing was that Jesus had turned out to be right about Babylon. It *hadn't* existed anymore; it was basically just empty desert with some parking lots, a few old buildings, and a lot of random debris. So that's what God blew up, shrieking down as he did: "No more dainties for you, whore! No more dainties! NO MORE *DAINTIES*!!" (NT, Rev. 18:14)

God later wondered whether this final dustup with Jesus had led him to the rather peculiar decision to marry Lamb-Jesus to the city of Jerusalem. (NT, Rev. 21:9–10) "That was bizarre, right, lion eyeball-monster? I mean, an animal marrying a city, that doesn't even make *sense*, does it?" It vaguely reminded God of when Solomon (that disloyal bastard) portrayed God as wanting to have sex with Jerusalem! "Which was absurd, obviously! Why would I want to have sex with a *city*, it doesn't make sense, how would you even do it?!" Fine, Jerusalem had had extremely attractive *thighs* (OT, Song 7:2) and also grape-cluster-like breasts (OT, Song 7:8–9)—or check that, even better, *deer*-like breasts! (OT, Song 7:4) Still, God didn't want to have intercourse with Jerusalem, that was a grotesque idea! (When people later described the "Song of Songs" as "wisdom literature," God shook his head and announced firmly: "I have another word for it: *Pornography*.")

CHAPTER TWENTY-SIX

After Judgment Day—big surprise—everything basically fell to shit. New Jerusalem (aka "Heaven on Earth") deteriorated quickly. With nothing to do other than pray, God's 144,000 Good Souls almost instantly seemed to get bored. On the rare occasions that God flew down to check up on them, he found hundreds of them curled up in fetal balls—moaning, beating their heads against walls, or trying to cut the "God" tattoo off their foreheads. (They couldn't do it because God had seen this coming and used permanent ink, haha.)

Before long, God's 144,000 Good Souls were cut in half . . . and then quartered . . . and within a decade, there were only a few thousand of them remaining (most of whom seemed to spend the majority of their time weeping.) Eventually, God dumped all of them in hell and New Jerusalem was empty once again—or nearly empty, that is. "Wizards and fornicators!" God bellowed angrily. "Why am I *still* plagued by wizards and fornicators?!" (NT, Rev. 22:15) Also: Why were there so many dogs gathered outside the gates of New Jerusalem? God loathed dogs. "The way they lick their own buttholes is *disgusting*," he had snarled on more than one occasion. (God despised cats too. "The way they *stare* at me is intolerable.") For a while, the wizards and perverts had giant sex parties in New Jerusalem and basically trashed it. After that, God sent his angels down to chop them all to pieces and bring their bodies back to heaven to feed to his eyeball-monsters.

As for heaven itself, it lasted a bit longer than New Jerusalem—but not by much. God's angels, as previously discussed, had quickly gone bad. Having essentially been created as "guard dogs" and with nothing left to guard, they had rapidly grown dangerous. Before long, God was hunting them down and killing them off by the thousands. Gabriel went missing one day and God never saw him again (until he choked him out, that is.) "Good riddance to bad garbage," God had muttered to himself at the time. As for his supposed "Wise Men," well, it turned out that pretty much all God liked about them was snapping their scrawny necks like dry branches.

As for Jesus—or, to be precise, the Jesuses—God quickly found himself wanting to be rid of them as soon as possible. Lamb Jesus had creeped God out by this point. Like Tanfoot Jesus, the Lamb had been getting older. Its eyes had turned milky and its horns had grown too long; they really should have been trimmed back—they'd actually started growing back into Lamb Jesus' head and it looked quite painful. God ended up luring Lamb Jesus into a firepit he'd dug and cooking him. (The meat had been tough, gamy, barely edible.) Baby Jesus, on the other hand, never seemed to grow any older; God didn't understand why, but the Baby had stayed approximately six months old, basically forever. God had suspected that Baby Jesus was there to "guilt" him somehow, but God never felt guilty about him, not in the least. As for Tanfoot Jesus, God had ended up bribing a few angels to betray him and take him out. (God paid the angels with literally the *last* source of beef in the entire universe: his cow eyeball-monster. That had been a hard day.) The angels told God that they'd killed Tanfoot Jesus—and it's true that God never saw Tanfoot again—but he definitely didn't think he was dead.

Anyway, no—God didn't miss the Jesuses. Nor did he miss his angels, nor his Wise Men. He didn't even miss his darling eyeball-monsters. He missed no one. The truth was, God felt *happy* to be alone again. It was exactly what he'd always wanted, he realized that now. He'd never enjoyed all the human drama, it had been exhausting. "This is perfect," God thought to himself. "No distractions. At long last I can think deeply about important things like ... mathematics and also ... hmm, yes, *philosophy*. At long last I can allow my all-knowing mind to ponder these subjects deeply, not to 'know' more, obviously, because that is patently impossible as I am already 'omniscient,' but rather to know all of the things that I didn't know I knew until I had the time to know I knew them! That's wonderful! Why, looking back, it almost seems *funny* to me that I created a universe at all! I so didn't *require* it! It probably looked to mankind like I somehow 'needed their love,' but that is absurd because I am perfect and therefore, by definition, in need of absolutely *nothing*."

"*You are perfect—perfect—perfect,*" the talking throne coos.

God stirs, opens his eyes. "*Perfect,*" the throne repeats over and over, stuck: "*You are perfect—perfect—perfect.*"

God shifts his weight, jabs an elbow back into the throne, trying to silence it. "*Perfect—perfect—perfect—perfect—perfect— perfect.*"

God lurches to his feet and stumbles away from the throne. Luckily, its voice is quiet and quickly recedes. Ten feet away, God stands in silence, hearing only the fast pounding of his heart.

"I am clearly *excited* by my endless future of alone-ness," he thinks to himself. "That is obviously why my heart is pounding so hard. I am not 'unnerved' by my situation in the least, that's a funny word to use—'unnerved'—I wonder why I even used it? Ah yes, of course, to be ironic. I'm obviously not on any level concerned about being alone forever and I *certainly* don't feel like *crying* about it, 'Boohoo, no one loves me and no one ever did?' Haha. *Please*."

God stands there, motionless for a very long time.

CHAPTER TWENTY-SEVEN

One day not too long afterward, God feels a presence near him. He spins around. Satan stands a few feet away, gazing at him. "What are *you* doing here?" God instantly demands of his eternal nemesis.

"I came to see you."

"How did you even *get* here?"

"I can go wherever I like. You must understand that by now."

God scowls. It's true: Satan can get into heaven, or anyplace else, any time he wants. "*Next* time," God thinks to himself, "I will set things up differently. Next time, I will create a way of actually *getting rid* of the wicked. Next time, I will create a cold and inescapable void of absolute darkness and silence which I will send the evil to." Lost in thought for a moment, God doesn't hear what Satan says. "What's that, devil?" God demands.

"I said: If a man digs a pit, he will fall into it."

"... *What?*"

"It's something your old friend Solomon once said." (OT, Ecc. 10:8)

"Yes, well, and it's utter nonsense. Now what do you *want* with me, Satan?"

Satan looks around, sighs. "You're alone, God."

God nods firmly. "That's right, Satan, I'm alone, exactly as I always wished to be. Exactly as I was at the start."

Satan studies God for a moment, then says something that literally makes God laugh aloud: "We never had a mother, God. That made things hard for us."

God shakes his head in scornful amusement. "A *mother*, Satan? A *MOTHER?* I think you've lost your mind, I really do, but for what it's worth, I didn't *need* a mother."

"Everyone needs a mother, God."

"Not me."

"Without a mother, things are much harder."

"Yes, well, as I said: Not for me, Satan, *not for me*."

"I'm trying to be a brother to you here, God."

Now God laughs even harder. "A *brother?* You truly *have* lost your mind haven't you, Satan? You're not my 'brother,' devil, you're my *creation,* I *created* you so that you could torment me, exactly as you have, well done!" God grins now, begins to openly mock Satan. "But wait—can it be? My god, yes, *now* I remember! You were in the darkness *with* me, weren't you, Satan? We were deserted in the void by our *mother*, that's right, and ohhhhh my goodness, apparently I was sooo traumatized by that experience that I created an entire reality out of my pain and rage and *that* explains why things went the way they did, doesn't it? What an epiphany! Thank you, Satan—or should I say 'brother'—thank you *so much!*"

Satan gazes at God until God's laughter finally subsides. "Why are you *looking* at me that way?" God demands sharply.

"You don't have much time left, God. That's what I came here to tell you."

"Not much *time* left? What on Earth are you talking about *now?* I have *eternity*, Satan."

Satan starts away. After a moment, God calls after him. "*Satan*."

Satan stops, looks back.

"*Stay out of my brain.*" Off Satan's blank look, God continues. "That 'inner voice' of mine, I know it's you. Stop doing it."

After Satan leaves, God feels extremely pleased about the way he's humiliated his nemesis. "He's an evil creature who knows nothing," God thinks to himself. "Honestly, he amuses me, he really does—some of those things he said—hahaha—were so utterly ridiculous—hahaha—"

God suddenly doubles over and begins to vomit. It goes on and on, as if God is trying to get something out of his system that simply does not want to come out.

That night, for the first time in a long time, God dreams of Jonah.

"*. . . wanted to forgive them,*" God murmurs heavily in his sleep. "*. . . wanted to forgive them all—even the one who didn't believe in me—even the animals. (OT, Jon. 4:11) . . . wanted to love everyone . . . wanted to love . . . but I didn't know how . . .*"

God awakes with a start.

There, standing ten feet away from him, is Jesus. Next to him is Satan. To their right is Mary. Behind them: Solomon . . . Moses . . . David . . . Abraham . . . Job . . . Noah . . . Adam and Eve . . . Gabriel . . . Behind them: hundreds, maybe thousands, more.

All standing and silently studying God.

"*Mary,*" God whispers. She looks away.

"Son," God manages. Jesus looks at him with his piercing eyes and suddenly God feels very ashamed of himself. "I'm sorry," he wants to say, "I'm so sorry." But he cannot, no, he simply cannot.

Satan looks at him and nods. "It's over now," God thinks to himself. "It's all over now."

EPILOGUE

God sits alone in the darkness. Around him: Nothing. A void. Absolute silence and stillness.

Feeling the heavy nothingness all around him, God's insides contract.

"Let there be light," he calls out.

Nothing happens.

A moment later he tries again, this time louder: "Let there be light!"

Still, nothing.

Now a third time, this time in a slightly higher-pitched voice: "Let there be *light*."

Nothing.

And finally a desperate whisper: *"Let there be light."*

Darkness.

ABOUT THE AUTHOR

Chris Matheson is the author of *The Story of God: A Biblical Comedy about Love (and Hate)*. He is also a screenwriter whose credits include *Bill & Ted's Excellent Adventure*, *Bill & Ted's Bogus Journey*, and *Rapture-Palooza*. He lives in Portland, Oregon.